Praise for *Square Waves*

"Romanoff understands that a great love story isn't just about who you want to be with—it's about who you want to be. (Okay, it's also about giddy flirtation, sharp banter, and hot sex.) I devoured it."

—Ann Friedman, journalist, essayist, and coauthor of *Big Friendship*

"Smart, steamy, and wickedly funny, this enemies-to-lovers romance had me hooked from page one. Cassidy and Leon's chemistry is hot, their banter is deliciously sharp, and I found myself laughing out loud one minute and fanning myself the next."

—Jo Piazza, best-selling author of *The Sicilian Inheritance*

"Romanoff is the antidote for romance readers who find themselves exhausted by romance books that follow the same script time and time again. *Square Waves* is the fresh, real, honest, raw romance that we've all been craving."

—Caro Chambers, best-selling author of *What to Cook When You Don't Feel Like Cooking*

Square Waves

ALEXANDRA ROMANOFF

831 STORIES

831 Stories

An imprint of Authors Equity
1123 Broadway, Suite 1008
New York, New York 10010

Copyright © 2025 by 831 Stories Inc.
All rights reserved.

Cover design by C47
Book design by Scribe Inc.

This is a work of fiction. Names, characters, places and incidents either are products of the author's imagination or are used fictitiously.

Library of Congress Control Number: 2025934717
Print ISBN 9798893310436
Ebook ISBN 9798893310498

Printed in the United States of America
First printing

www.831stories.com
www.authorsequity.com

To my therapists, past and present

WEEK ONE

1

I haven't lived here in a decade, but my parents have kept my childhood bedroom a time capsule: a preserved-in-amber reminder of who I used to be Before. The white lace curtains on the windows are sweet and girly; the vanity mirror has photo booth snapshots of me with high school girlfriends tucked into its frame. There's a literal blue ribbon hanging above the bed, a souvenir of the academic merit award I won as a senior. All the markings of exactly who I was: the kind of girl people love.

I rarely think about that version of me anymore. For the first twenty-two years of my life, Cassidy Weaver wasn't a household name or one synonymous with scandal. But I've been After Cassidy for long enough that that can be hard to recall. Unless, of course, I'm thrust back into rooms where I used to spend most of my time focused on English homework and extracurriculars that looked good on early decision applications.

In so many ways, I know myself better now than I did then. And one thing I'm certain of is that if I don't unpack tonight, I'll spend the next three weeks living out of a suitcase. I force myself from the edge of the bed to the closet, open its door, and groan. How is there still clothing in here? Didn't I take everything with me when I moved to DC for college?

As I scan the relics, I allow myself a moment of tenderness for this former self and her miniskirts so mini, they might as well be belts. Band T-shirts from my short-lived emo phase hang above pairs of *very* aspirationally high heels.

Then I shove it all to the side and start hanging my things—my current things. The Char cashmere sweater I bought with my first big paycheck, the boots I've had resoled three times, and the Issey Miyake dress that will probably always be my best-ever thrift find. I wish I saw the contrast between these two wardrobes as reassuring: a reminder of all of the years that have passed since I lived here. How much I've survived and even grown. But the things I've packed feel like they're from another life too. One I'm not entirely sure I want anymore.

One that might not want me either.

Once I've slid my suitcase under the bed, I give in to the teenage gravity of the room and flop down on my old comforter. When I free my phone from my back pocket, there are no new messages. The last person I heard from was my mom, alerting me that she and my dad were on the plane, headed to Paris for their thirtieth anniversary celebration. *The house is going to be so happy to see you!!* she wrote.

I tap a thumbs-up reply and then unreply and replace it with a heart instead.

SQUARE WAVES

Technically, all I have to do this month is unpack my bags in my parents' Berkeley Craftsman. Starting Friday when I left the office, I officially kicked off the minisabbatical that my boss didn't suggest as much as ordered. It turns out I wasn't the only one to notice my thoughts shifting from *I wonder if I'm burning out* to *I physically cannot make myself function at work*. This break was framed as a gift, but we both know there was an underlying message: *Take a few weeks, get yourself together . . . and if you don't, don't come back.*

My parents aren't aware of the unstated threat. They only know the story that I've been telling them, which is that the time off is a reward for an intense-but-gratifying job well done. I've already consumed my fair share of sympathy and can't risk eliciting more. I have zero desire to see pity on anyone's face ever again if I can help it.

I shift onto my back and fight my first yawn. I'm trapped in that weird in-between time of oncoming jet lag. It's 11 p.m. where I came from but 8 p.m. here. Too early to go to sleep, but my eyelids are getting heavy anyway.

I need to get out of this house if I want to stay awake, but I don't have a lot of options. I've already eaten—my mom left me a square of lasagna in the fridge, which I consumed standing up in the kitchen as soon as I walked through the door.

But . . . a bar, maybe? A drink sounds nice. An adult activity, a reminder that I'm not actually eighteen anymore. And who knows? Maybe I'll meet someone hot. Have a flirtation.

I laugh out loud, alone by myself. Berkeley guys come in three types—nerdy grad student, nerdy techie, and nerdy professor—and none of them are mine. But I roll off the bed, put on my favorite jeans and some mascara, and grab my parents' keys anyway.

There's a mirror hanging above their entryway, and as I head out, I catch a glimpse of myself: my blonde hair in its messy topknot, my cheeks pale because, despite the fact that it's deep summer, I haven't spent an afternoon outside in ages. I look as tired as I feel. But that's fine. I'm not going anywhere fancy. Mostly, getting a cocktail will waste away an hour. And what am I doing here if not killing time?

I haven't lived in Berkeley in a long time and never when I could legally drink, so I have to consult the Infatuation about where to even go. I decide on a comfortingly divey place that, on Sunday night, is busy but not packed. Almost as soon as I slide onto an empty seat at the bar, a bartender comes over to take my order. She has a tragus piercing and a complicated haircut. It's cliché but true: the Bay Area is *so* different from DC. And I have missed it here.

"Do you know what you want?" she asks.

I bite my lip, like this is a trick question. In college, I drank vodka sodas; AC (After Cooper) I learned that that was a sorority girl tell and switched to gin and tonics. But my go-to doesn't feel like the right thing for this moment. It suddenly seems so . . . East Coast blasé. But then what *do* I want? A beer? A glass of wine? Is this a celebratory drink or a mournful one, and how do I even—

My ruminating is interrupted by a hand on my shoulder.

A man's voice near my ear, low and pleased with itself. "Do you need help ordering, Cassidy?"

I whirl around and find myself face-to-face—uncomfortably close, nose-tip-to-nose-tip, he-can-probably-smell-my-breath close—with Leon Park.

The first thing my traitor brain thinks is, *Handsome.* Which, to be fair, is an accurate reaction to Leon's presence. He was hot in high school, and he's even hotter now. His thick black hair has grown out into perfectly tousled waves. His eyes are still amber and still sparkling. He smirks at me, and it's equal parts disarming and infuriating. I'm both grateful and annoyed that I tried even a little bit before coming here tonight.

Thank god he drops his hand and steps back, creating some distance between us so that I have room for a second thought: *Oh, Jesus Christ, no.*

It wouldn't be fair to say that Leon and I were nemeses back in the day because that would indicate that he cared about me. But we did annoy the shit out of each other, our opposite personalities creating friction every time we so much as spoke. I would have avoided him if I could, but my teenage best friend Willa dated his best friend Zeke for *all four years of Berkeley High* . . . only to break up a few weeks after graduation, when it was too late to do me any good.

It's been almost a decade since I've been in Leon's proximity, but his presence kicks me into gear, and I hear the words "I'll have a martini" coming out of my mouth before I have a chance to consider the thought.

A martini? Where the hell did that come from?

The bartender reaches for a glass. "Vodka or gin?" she asks.

"Gin." At least this part I know. "Botanist, if you have it."

"Sure. How dry do you want it?"

"Oh. Um. Medium dry?"

"Olives?"

My neck goes hot. What is this, the Spanish Inquisition? "Sure."

She looks over at Leon. "And you?"

"I'll have a PBR, please."

I know he's just ordering a beer, but it still feels like he's trying to show me up by getting something simple and unfussy that doesn't require a litany of follow-up questions. Leon is the chillest bro ever to chill. And I am *not*. That's one thing that Before Cassidy and After Cassidy have in common: an inability to live up to every California girl's birthright and just, like, go with the flow, man.

Leon turns so that his back is against the bar. He props himself up on his elbows and stretches his long legs out in front of him. His jeans are so worn, they're almost—but not quite—ripping at the knees, and his Vans are authentically skate-scuffed. His eyelashes are soot black against his cheeks as he blinks at me.

"What are you doing here?" he asks.

I look for accusation in his tone, but he actually sounds curious. I'm still not letting my guard down. "Having a drink."

"Oh, so we're being *literal* tonight."

"What else would we be?"

"Excuse me for making conversation."

I can't help it: I roll my eyes. "Since when do you want to talk to me in the first place?"

"Cass. Please." Only people who know me from Before call me Cass. I correct everyone else, to ward off any creep toward unearned intimacy.

Leon smiles like he means it, and a pinprick of a dimple forms on his right cheek. There's a corresponding uptick in my heart rate. God*damnit*. I hate this guy for a lot of reasons, and the way my body responds to his has always been one of them.

He slips a hand into his front pocket. "Anyway, I could ask you the same question."

Before I can consider his response, the bartender is back with our drinks. My glass looks unwieldy, a clear, shallow pond of gin sitting atop a long, thin stem, and I wish again that I'd ordered something else. Maybe Leon will leave me to go meet up with friends? Or some sun-bleached Instagram model with a surfboard strapped to her truck and a side gig reading tarot cards?

But my luck has always been shitty, and he hops up onto the barstool next to mine.

"Well, to answer the question you didn't ask, I live here," he says. "Same as I always have."

"So is this your local?" Because of course I would walk into his regular haunt.

"Nah. I was supposed to meet up with Zeke, actually, but he bailed last minute. I was already halfway here, so I figured may as well." He gestures at the baseball game on the TV, and I watch the shape of his shoulder moving under his T-shirt. Leon was skinny in high school, all limbs. He's still got some of that teenage lankiness about him, even though we're nearing thirty.

"So you and Zeke are still close."

"Yeah. We try, anyway. He had a kid last year, and it's—he's a really good dad. But his wife works nights, so it's just . . . getting time with him is hard."

"Holy shit. Zeke's a dad." The idea makes me a little dizzy. If Zeke is already that kind of adult . . . I try not to play the comparison game, but I am toeing the starting line.

"Does he still have—" I gesture at my hair. In high school, Zeke's trademark was a gelled mohawk, always dyed the loudest possible colors: sunset pink or fluorescent orange.

"Nah. Kept it for the wedding just to prove a point, but it's too much maintenance. It's buzzed down super tight right now. You might not recognize him anymore. He just looks like a regular guy."

I'm too stunned to say more than "God, I guess we are grown-ups."

"Sure are, Ms. Martini." Leon's tone is a little too pointed. There goes that nice nostalgic moment we were having.

"It's just a cocktail."

"And you haven't touched it."

I haven't. The glass is precariously full; I have no idea how the bartender got it over here without spilling. Under other circumstances, I would just slurp some directly off the surface, but not in front of Leon. I refuse to let him see me as anything less than adept.

So instead, I pick it up delicately and raise it to my mouth in slow motion, my lips pursed. I know I must look ridiculous. It takes what feels like a full minute for me to manage a sip.

When I do, it tastes cold and floral and salinated. Perfect. I put the glass back down and close my eyes for a second.

When I open them, I expect Leon to mock me for something—my pincer grip on the stem, maybe—but he's just . . . looking at me. His gaze is glued to my mouth. I know it's not possible, but I'd swear his irises are a few shades darker.

"Good?" he asks.

"Yeah."

Leon looks away and takes a long pull on his beer. "So you still haven't told me what you're doing here. Are you not going to answer simple questions tonight?"

"I don't think I am." As childish as it is, I can't help but enjoy getting a rise out of him. There was a time when the only thing that could shake Leon from his lazy surfer posture was getting irritated with me. That kind of power is hard to resist.

"Will you answer complicated questions, then?"

"What's a complicated question? Like, you want my thoughts on Bay Area housing? For me to weigh in on the political issues of the day?" I wince as soon as I say it. I very specifically *don't* want to talk politics with Leon or anyone. It's way too easy to jump from someone's opinion of President Knight's second term to the scandal that almost kept him from getting elected in the first place.

Wasn't that when Cooper Abbot fucked his wife's college intern?

Wasn't that intern . . . me?

I'm anticipating a sharp retort. But Leon sighs and shakes his head. "You know, it's actually been kind of a long day," he says. "So if I were going to ask you a complicated question, Cassidy, it might be: Why does it seem like you hate me so much? Still?"

I'm startled. Obviously Leon knows I don't like him. It's not hard to miss. But the way he says it—I don't know. It almost sounds like he *cares*.

"I don't hate you" is all I can muster, even if it isn't true. "And once again, I could ask you—"

"You could," he says. "But I asked you first."

He shifts toward me slightly, and I catch a whiff of his scent: Old Spice and skin. I'm hit between the eyes with a memory from over a decade ago: a summer evening at the beach, a bonfire burning. Leon and a bunch of boys stripping off their shirts and sprinting into the ocean screaming. How they ran back, drenched, and launched themselves at us, the knot of girls gossiping on a blanket. Leon landed half on top of me, and the water streaming off him was freezing, but he was warm. He smelled exactly the same then, and I still remember the twist I felt in my stomach. The rush between my legs.

He's giving me a perfect opening to say something smart, or mean, or both. And I'm tempted to take it. To pick up my less perilously full glass and just walk away.

But the truth is, for the last six years, everyone in the world has had an opinion about me. Some people think I'm an evil slut who destroyed an innocent man's career with her wiles; some people think I'm a victim of the patriarchy who needs to be saved. But they're all working off a media narrative—articles they read or podcasts they listened to. I've contributed to some of that with my work with the nonprofit Kindness Is Better, or KIB, sometimes penning my own op-eds and doing public speaking. I've made being Cassidy Weaver, "Gen Z's Monica Lewinsky," my entire career and a good chunk of my actual life.

But Leon actually knows me. Knew me, at least. Whatever he doesn't like about me is hard-earned.

An unwelcome thought: *If only you didn't despise him so much, he really would be the perfect hookup.*

I mentally bat it away and take another sip of my drink before responding. If I was less tired, I might be able to come up with something clever. But I only have it in me to tell the truth. "Okay, well. You didn't like me. So I didn't like you back."

Leon raises an eyebrow. "When did I give you that impression?"

As if he's completely innocent here. "Oh, I don't know, when you made fun of my seventh-grade history presentation grade for being *too detailed*." Instantly, my cheeks go hot. I can't believe he goaded me into admitting that I'm still hung up on some barb from half a lifetime ago. But it was the first semester of middle school, when impressions mattered deeply. Plus, I might have already developed a tiny crush on Leon. To have him notice me but only to make fun of me—well. Clearly it left a mark.

For some reason, he doesn't seize the opportunity to

tease me. "Why did you care what I thought?" His elbow moves closer to mine. "I almost failed that class."

I narrow my eyes. I knew Leon wasn't a hardworking student, but he always gave off the aura of being so smart that he didn't have to study. I assumed he got effortless A's and that if he didn't, it was because he was too cool to care about something as lame as grades.

"People like boys who fail way better than girls who succeed," I say with a shrug. At the time, it felt like he was putting a target on my back, pointing out to everyone, *This one tries too hard*. And of course, because I am who I am, I only doubled down after that. And I went even harder when Leon was around.

"That's true."

I'm so surprised to hear him agreeing with me—about anything, even something as obvious as the basic dynamics of sexism—that I drink half my martini in a single gulp. "Be careful," I quip, sliding the olive from its skewer. "Next thing you know you'll be apologizing to me."

"Do you want me to?"

I squint at Leon, and I feel like I actually see him for the first time all night. He's sun-browned, his skin darker than it ever was in high school, in a way that makes me wonder if he works outside. When he smiles, crow's-feet crinkle at the corners of his eyes. He's wearing a long-sleeved shirt, and it's shoved up on one muscular forearm; I see the edge of a tattoo there, a suggestion of all the ways he might have changed in the last ten years that aren't visible to me yet.

If we were strangers, just meeting, I would be following

the thing I feel between us: this gentle, insistent desire to get closer. I would be angling my body toward his. Maybe our legs would brush or I would touch his thigh.

The next steps are well trod. Immediately after Cooper, I was depressed, and then for a while, I was reckless. I slept with anyone I wanted to and some people I kind of didn't. I know exactly how to map the route from a barstool to a bedroom.

But Leon and I are not strangers. Hardly. Which makes this even more precarious . . . and, in some ways, even more enticing.

I lean an elbow on the bar, put my chin in my hand. My drink is mostly gone, and I feel loose. Relaxed for the first time in months.

"What would a Leon Park apology even look like?"

He smiles at me, huge, dimple on full display. "It would look like me saying, 'I'm sorry, Cassidy.'" He reaches out and pats my knee. My breath catches in my throat, and I think he notices because he leaves his palm there just a half second too long. Like maybe he's gauging my reaction.

Like maybe he wants to keep touching me.

"I appreciate that."

"Honey, you want another one?" the bartender cuts in.

My gaze is locked on Leon, and if I was feeling like myself, I would say no. I would think, *Go home, Cassidy*, and then do it.

But between burnout and jet lag, gin and desire, the last six years and the last twelve hours, I'm not entirely sure who *myself* is. So instead, I say, "Yes, please."

II

An hour, another drink, and a shared basket of fries later, Leon and I are both tipsy. We're also still talking. We've somehow managed to avoid the *What have you been up to?* chatter that kills most of my catch-up conversations with high school classmates. Instead, we've walked ourselves into an exaggerated debate about whether or not it's a betrayal that, while living in DC for six years, I've gotten into baseball . . . only to become a Nationals fan.

"But I didn't *ever* like the Giants," I say. I've pivoted on my stool, and so has Leon. One of my knees is pressed firmly against his, and it's becoming increasingly challenging to focus on anything else. "So I don't owe them anything."

"It's not just the Giants! It's the whole Bay Area! That's your *hometown team*." He throws his hands up at my disloyalty.

"I feel like you should be happy that I'm into baseball at all. That I speak your language." I down the last of my second martini.

Leon shakes his head. "Cassidy, not that much has changed since you last saw me. Sports is hardly *my language*."

"So why do you care whether or not I root for the Giants?"

He rubs his jaw. "My ex got me into them," he says. "She sold it as a way to connect to the whole city. To make yourself a part of something bigger. Something collective."

"Your ex, huh?" That I manage to ask this without shame is a sign of how far we've come at this bar. I don't know if that's a good omen or a bad one.

"Yeah. We broke up last year."

I do the mental math. It's August now; at a minimum, that's eight months ago. Is he technically still on the rebound at this point? And do I care?

"What about you?" Leon takes the final sip of his beer. "Is that why you're here? Hiding out from a terrible breakup?" He knocks his knee against mine, and it slips forward so that the bone presses against the inside of my thigh. My focus shifts to the sensation of pressure and how good it would feel sliding up between my legs. My mouth goes dry at the thought.

"No."

"So you're single." His T-shirt is loose at the neck, and when he leans forward to talk to me, I can see the line of his collarbone, the hints of more tattoos. Hangul, I think.

Laughter from a few barstools down distracts me from my ogling. "Last time I checked," I say. *I have been single for six straight years now*, I don't say.

Leon drags a fingertip through the condensation on the outside of his glass. Dots a bead of water onto the bar top, and then another. I wish it wasn't mesmerizing.

"I don't like being single," he says wistfully.

We've stayed pretty close to the surface so far, and that's my comfort zone, socially. This conversational turn is more personal than I expected, and I'm surprised by how pleased I am that Leon's opening the door to it.

"Why not?"

"I was with my ex for two years, and right after we broke up, I felt like I had so much autonomy. So much free *time*. But now, I don't know. I miss Tuesday nights on the couch with someone. And I miss—" He cuts himself off abruptly, darts his eyes at a corner of the room.

Is Leon really not going to say it? "Sex," I supply matter-of-factly. "You miss sex."

As soon as the words are out of my mouth, I understand why he stopped short. All night, I've been trying—and mostly failing—to ignore the simmer of attraction I feel toward him. Now I feel like I've shown my cards.

Leon doesn't miss it either. His smile gets smaller, more dangerous. "Yes." There's a low rumble in his voice. "I do miss sex, Cass."

I'm so thrown by how turned on I am that I've basically lost control of my mouth. "That's a surprise."

He raises an eyebrow, holds it there. I feel like a mouse being toyed with by a cat.

"I mean, I just . . . I feel like you're always—" I gesture toward his torso with my hands. It occurs to me that Leon and I have never had a conversation this long before. Maybe because I sensed that if we did, I'd find myself in exactly this position.

"Always what?"

"Nothing."

"Always what, Cassidy?" Another nudge with his knee, another thrum in my stomach.

Of course he's going to make me say it. "You know." I play with the stem of my empty glass just to have something to do. "Girls were always falling in your lap."

Leon runs his fingers through his hair. It has flecks of something in it—maybe paint? "Not sure about that. And anyway, I didn't know you were paying attention."

"It was hard not to." I realize too late that I sound sulky, envious. Leon's girlfriends were an endless roster of silky-haired stoners he'd met at skate parks and in surf lineups, each of them more carefree and effortless than the last.

Leon considers this, and I wonder if I've given myself away. I jump in before he can decipher too much. "I get it though." There are warning bells going off in my head, but I barely hear them. I try to sound nonchalant when I say, "Longing for sex. Even when it's not so far out of reach." My gaze locks with his, and my breath catches. Heat blazes between my hipbones. And I can't make myself look away.

"In high school, you always seemed too good for it," Leon says, his eyes transfixed, as though he's afraid to blink. "Like you weren't obsessively horny like the rest of us. I always sort of wondered what it would take to make you—"

My mouth has fallen open, I realize, and I force my jaw shut. I'm so much less bold than I used to be Before, less stupid and selfish too. But some things never change. Leon's admission seems genuine, but it also has the distinct ring of someone throwing down a challenge. And I always rise to meet those.

"You could find out. If you wanted to."

Leon's eyes go wider, and his breath catches audibly, like he's choking on air. No matter what happens next, the satisfaction of getting that reaction out of him will have been worth it.

I watch him swallow. Shift in his seat. When he can speak again, he sputters out, "You mean . . . okay, yeah."

I shrug, like it doesn't make a difference to me one way or the other. "I wasn't planning on getting another drink, so . . ."

He's already signaling to the bartender for the check, and as we wait, my brain catches up to what's happening and starts reminding me why this is a terrible idea. What the fuck did I just propose? I'm going to sleep with *Leon Park*? Sure, he seems different than when we were eighteen, but he's still mildly arrogant and extremely irritating and way too handsome, and if our high school friends ever find out, I will *never* live this down.

Leon interrupts my racing thoughts with a touch: his hand, heavy and warm, on the small of my back. I turn into him instinctively, just as the bartender slides two separate bills in front of us. For this, I am grateful. It's a good reminder of what this is between us. And what it isn't.

"Just to be clear, this doesn't mean anything," I tell Leon anyway, signing my name with a flourish.

He leans down to whisper in my ear, his hand still warm on me. "Oh, don't worry. I know."

III

When we exit to the parking lot, it's chilly like it always is in the Bay, even in August. Fog is starting to roll in to blanket the city as the night gets deeper.

Leon nods toward a bike chained up in front. "That's my ride, so let me call an Uber, yeah?"

I glance toward the CR-V I drove here, brand new and borrowed from my parents. No way do I trust my two-martini, about-to-have-sex-with-Leon self to drive it. "Thanks," I say as I adjust to the new surroundings, the two of us plucked from our bubble at the bar.

I watch as Leon taps at his phone, biting his lower lip in concentration as he tells it where we are and where we want to go. My mind wanders to where it is I want *him* to go. Where I want his hands, his mouth. The idea of finally touching him—of having all of his attention on me and getting him to do what I want—it's a little overwhelming.

He puts his phone back in his pocket, rakes a hand through his hair. His shirt slides up so that I can see the cut of his hipbone and smooth skin below his navel.

He catches me looking. My instinct is to deny it—to

make a joke—but then I remember that it's too late for that. So I meet his gaze, defiant.

Leon's mouth curls into a grin. "Oh," he says. "Okay. I can work with that."

Then he walks me back until I'm pressed against the outer wall of the bar. Its stucco is cold against my back. He cages me in with his arms, one palm pressed flat on either side of my head. For a second I think he's about to say something else, but he doesn't.

He kisses me instead.

On the rare occasions when I would let myself imagine something like this happening, I always assured myself that it would be terrible. That Leon would be the stereotypical pretty boy: lazy and self-involved in bed. He would be too accustomed to women desperate to make him feel good to know how to make me feel good.

But he kisses me like it matters—insistently but with care. I wind my arms around him and feel more than hear his groan when my fingers tangle in his hair. I've been wet for what feels like hours now, since the second he first touched me, and I arch up into the palm he runs down my neck before he cups my breast with one hand, then my ass with the other. A hurt little sound escapes me, something pleading and way too raw.

When Leon pulls away, I worry I've overdone it already, but then I realize our car is here, a nondescript Toyota Corolla idling at the curb. The driver is looking very hard at his phone.

"Uh . . ." Leon's mouth is red; his tongue traces his lower

lip, and I wonder if he can taste me there, gin and spit and want. "You ready?"

I've been ready for way too long. "Yeah. Yes." He guides me toward the car with a more gentlemanly flourish than I knew he possessed.

He only lives twenty minutes away, somewhere in Oakland, naturally, but every minute feels like an hour. I don't let myself think any what-if thoughts or look at him. I don't trust that I won't straddle him in the backseat if I do. Instead, I watch the night blur by outside and try to keep my heart from beating out of my chest.

When we pull to a stop, I try to decode Leon's house, a rambling Victorian that's way too big for just one person. "We're a no-shoes place," he says in the entryway, pointing to a rack. A roommate then. Probably more than one. I kick off my flats while he unties his sneakers and wheels his bike into its corner.

He grabs my hand, silently steering me through a cozy-looking living room and kitchen and up a back staircase. Something about it feels like we're sneaking around, and I have to admit that only adds to the allure.

His bedroom is cluttered but tidy. Organized chaos. His bedframe is so low to the ground that for a second, I'm not sure he has one. The walls are layered with posters and paintings and prints of photographs. I walk over to take a closer look, but before I can really see much of anything, Leon wraps his arms around me, hooking his chin over my shoulder.

I spin to face him. He hasn't bothered turning the lamps

on, but the moon is full and bright, making the room feel like a pencil sketch of itself. In the shadowy light, it's easier to imagine that Leon is a stranger, someone with whom I can successfully pull off a one-night stand.

He kisses my neck, and I tilt my head back reflexively, baring my throat. He's all heat and tongue and teeth, and my pulse is throbbing, every part of me trying to get closer to his mouth. He moves lower, kissing my collarbone, then dipping between my breasts through my clothes. When he sinks to his knees, I suck in a breath. I'm undone by the sight, by the way he runs his hands up my hips, under my sweater, skating his palms across the skin of my stomach.

"Come here," he says, hands firmly on my waist. I sink down onto the bed, pulling him on top of me.

Leon kisses me once, twice, before he raises up and pulls his shirt over his head with one hand. He has a distinct farmer's tan, his torso several shades paler than his arms or his face; he's even more muscular than his clothed frame lets on. Like he puts his body to use. And I can finally see the tattoos I wondered about earlier—a half-abstract design that circles his forearm and winds up his bicep and then across his shoulders before morphing into Hangul letters across his right pec.

I sit up and tug my own shirt off. My boobs are nothing to write home about, but Leon responds with a gratifying grunt and presses me back down, tugging them out of my bra and licking and nipping hungrily. I gasp at his gusto, his fervor, and my hands are in his hair again. I am arching into his touch, helpless. I can't remember the last time

I felt this far out of my head and fully in my body. I only have one thought: *More*.

My pulse is mostly in my clit when I flip us over and start toying with the fly on his jeans. He doesn't say anything, just watches me. For a moment he looks like a boy again, wide-eyed with wonder. But then he remembers himself and smirks.

I want to wipe any self-satisfaction off his face. So I open his fly, pull him out of his underwear, and drop my head, licking the beads of precum that have formed on his tip before I take all of him in my mouth. The thrilling sensation of his dick hitting the back of my throat extends all the way to my toes. I moan with contentment and feel his body tense in response to the vibration.

Comment-section creeps almost ruined giving head for me. My big sex scandal was getting fucked on a senator's desk, not giving Oval Office–adjacent blow jobs, but no one can ever remember that when making stale jokes about kneepads and DSLs on Reddit. And for a while I was worried that stuff like that was all anyone would ever be thinking about in a moment like this one.

But Leon just sighs my name: "Cass." He's known me for so long, and it feels completely right to taste him, salt and musk and skin on my tongue. To sink my mouth down and let him watch me swallow him over and over again.

Leon's thighs start to tremble, and I wonder how close he is. I pull off and look up at him, and I trust I look unbearably smug when I ask, "As good as you imagined?"

He responds by hooking his hands behind my knees

and flipping me onto my back so that my head is hanging off the edge of his bed. I'm about to protest, but before I can, Leon's hand is between my legs, the heel of it sliding over my flesh, and he can feel exactly how wet he's made me. "Fuck, Cass, it's like that, huh?" he says into my jaw as he slides two fingers inside of me, curling his knuckles and circling his thumb against my clit. I grip the sheets, but my hold does nothing to quell my shaking.

"That's it," he murmurs. "That's it, baby." I'm too far gone to bristle at the use of a pet name. "Come on, Cass. Let me see it. Let me see you fall apart."

Those words bring me crashing back into myself. The orgasm that was starting to feel inevitable recedes like the tide. *Falling apart* means something different to me than it does to a lot of people, and it's not for others to see. I can't let Leon witness me boneless, putty in his hands.

So I wrap my fingers around his wrist, even though it pains me to do it. "Stop," I breathe. "I don't want to come yet. I want you inside of me when I do." I know I won't get any pushback to that.

Another grunt, the sound involuntary. His jaw tightens.

We pull away from each other just long enough to get completely naked and for him to grab a condom. Then he kneels over me and gives himself a few strokes before he slides it on. Watching him is . . . mesmerizing. His dick is thick, and I can still feel its heaviness on my tongue. My brain almost skipped the tracks back there, but now it's reasserting itself, my desire coming back online.

When I bracket Leon's hips with my legs, he wastes no

time, sinking forward, sliding into me, and stretching me open in one slow, perfect thrust that blacks out the concept of *thoughts* completely. I don't know which one of us gasps; maybe it's both. "Jesus Christ," he whispers, strands of his hair framing my face as he looks down at me with an expression of wonder. I've had a lot of sex, but I don't know if I've ever felt anything like this, this simultaneous want for him to *move* and to have him stay here, as far inside of my body as he can get for a very, very long time.

I don't have to choose. Leon fucks me steadily, pulling out only to drive back in again. I feel something building low in my gut, the ache of the orgasm I denied both of us earlier.

It keeps growing, getting sharper and stronger with each rock of our bodies. He reaches down to touch my clit again and smiles softly, his lower lip between his teeth, when he sees how much I like it. I can't help my body's reactions, and I don't want to. I can sense I'm being loud, and I'm too lost to care. But I still can't quite imagine letting Leon watch me come.

So I dig my fingers into his ass, rolling him to his side and wordlessly rearranging myself on my hands and knees. I turn to look at him, gesturing with my head to indicate what I want, and as soon as he can, Leon is pressing himself inside me again, hands like a brand on either side of my hips. I mash my face against his pillow and finally, finally give up on doing anything other than feeling. I embrace what I've always liked best about sex: the ability to stop thinking, to be just a body for a few minutes. Skin and sweat and want.

He slides his hands from my hips up my sides, one

landing on my breast and the other wrapping gently around my throat. It's possessive, almost animalistic, and the fact that it feels so out of character for our dynamic only turns me on more.

When I come, the sensation rakes across me like nails, sharp and stinging. Underneath that, a more lingering pleasure blooms and aches like a bruise. I'm pretty sure I shout. I return to myself with my mouth open, panting, against the cotton of Leon's pillowcase. My neck is damp, and my body pulses with aftershocks, trembling in time with my heartbeat.

I'm practically limp as he presses into me one last time, his hips stuttering as he comes. All I can hear is the soft suck of his breath—half a gasp—and I realize that I've played myself. Maybe letting him witness my orgasm would have been worth being able to see his: Leon Park, unguarded, earnest, totally committed.

Maybe next ti—I shove the thought out of my mind. There will not be a next time. This was a little self-indulgent one-off. A question has been answered. It doesn't have to mean anything other than I needed to feel something, we were both sexually restless, and he's unfortunately still hot.

I tell myself all of this while I gather up my clothes and reach for my phone to order a ride.

"You don't—" Leon starts, then stops.

"Hm?" My back is turned to him as I tug on my jeans.

"Oh, just . . . I don't know. Do you need anything? Water, or . . . ?"

"Nope. Car's on its way. Does the front door lock automatically?"

"Yeah," he says. "It does."

He sounds almost . . . dismayed, and I can't help myself from turning to look at him. I'm prepared to gloat that we're ending this interaction with me fully clothed and him with his soft dick out, but his face is open and tired in a way I've never seen before. "It's been real, Leon," I say with less edge than I intend.

He laughs. "It's been very real, Cassidy."

I bite back a smile. I want to say something else, but everything I come up with sounds like an invitation—*See you around*—or too corny—*Take care*. So instead, I settle for one last look at him. His hair is a wreck, and his mouth is red from mine. His dick *is* soft, but it doesn't look stupid, somehow; it looks—

I walk myself to the door to leave before I can do anything truly dumb, like ask if I can stay so we can do it again in the morning.

IV

I resist waking up for a long time. Being conscious means I have to remember how to be a real person again. Someone who thinks about words like *consequences* and *the future*.

When I finally admit to myself that it's time to roll out of bed, I open all of the curtains to let what sunlight there is spill into the house. Then I take a long, hot shower. My skin is tender from Leon's touch, even though he didn't leave a single mark.

It's Monday, and I feel compelled to do something that at least resembles work. Getting dressed, I still can't quite believe that I need a sweatshirt, especially since the fog hasn't entirely burned off yet. It was almost ninety degrees in DC yesterday, humidity so thick it felt like dew against my skin. But in the Bay, it's downright chilly.

Driving to the bar last night, I felt like it could have been anywhere, the city anonymous in the dark. But in daylight, it's inescapable: Here I am again. Back where I started.

I pack up my laptop and head to a newer coffee shop, the kind of hip, minimalist-modern place that didn't exist yet when I was growing up. I'm glad to have the shame factor of being in public to keep me from looking up Leon to see if he's on Instagram. Instead, I open a blank Google Doc and type the words *Game Plan*.

Then I stare at them while my coffee gets cold. What the fuck do I do next?

That question has been answered for me basically ever since Cooper Abbot appeared in Senator Knight's campaign office for the third time in a week and said, "Cassidy, right?" I was twenty-two, about to graduate college, and scared out of my mind about the lack of direction I had for my future. I had thought DC might be a good place to be ambitious, but I didn't actually like working on the campaign all that much; I hadn't especially liked any of my previous internships either. What I did like was the way I felt when Cooper—polished, successful, charismatic—looked at me like I was worth paying attention to. So I followed that impulse straight into a national scandal that landed my name on the front page of *The Washington Post*.

From there, my options were practically nonexistent. Who would hire me? I spent a miserable nine months depressed and underemployed in DC, scared that fleeing to California would only cement my banishment. On a day when I was sure I had already hit rock bottom, I went out for coffee and ran into Maya McPherson—Cooper's by-then ex-wife, the woman he'd been cheating on during our affair. I'd braced myself for the private version of the lashing I'd been given publicly, but it never came. She was profoundly, almost radically, empathetic, and ultimately she was the one who turned my life around. A few months after our run-in, Maya connected me with KIB, and the nonprofit hired me as an ambassador: a spokeswoman who could share authentically and openly about my experiences with cyberbullying.

At first it seemed cynical. And if I'd had any other opportunities, I wouldn't have taken it. I didn't want to make money off something that I shouldn't have done in the first place. But the more I actually did the work, the more meaningful I found it. Even if I couldn't forgive myself yet—that would take years, or is still taking years, honestly—I felt deeply for the people I met on the job: people who would approach me to tell their stories. Say that my bravery had made them brave. I never *felt* brave, but for them, I could at least make believe. And the pretending felt worthwhile.

Ironically, continuing to put myself in the public eye meant that I would never *stop* being cyberbullied. I learned to turn off comments where I could and not read them when I couldn't. I deleted all of my social media the day a photo of me from a college party, looking very blonde, round-cheeked, and scantily clad, was pulled from my own Instagram account, published in the newspaper, and subsequently attached to my Wikipedia entry.

Still, snide remarks and stand-up jokes managed to leak in around the edges. That combined with the vulnerability required to work with the vulnerable wore me down, like metal corroding over time. Lately, that exhaustion had started showing up in my performance on the job, until finally, my boss gave me the nicest ultimatum she could:

"I think it's time for you to decide if it's still worth it to you to do this work."

I know which way I'm leaning, at least in theory. The problem is that if I don't have this, I have no idea what I have.

I pull my chair closer to the café table and rest my fingers on the keyboard. Just start. In desperation, I list out jobs. Not ones I want, just ones that exist. *Doctor. Lawyer. Barista. Professor. Bike messenger.* But all this does is remind me that I've never been clear on what I wanted to be when I grew up. It's the same disorienting feeling I've gotten perusing LinkedIn job listings. Companies want administrative assistants with master's degrees or communications specialists with decades of experience. People who know what they're doing. There are no requests for someone in their late twenties with a bachelor's in political science whose main area of expertise is being themself.

I'm in a truly black mood when I drive home for my virtual therapy appointment. I've been seeing Dr. Tilly Renolds once a week for the past six years, and she's not about to let me skip a session just because I'm on the other side of the country. Sometimes, I wish we hadn't all learned to use Zoom.

When I log on, I try to keep my face neutral. "How's California?" asks Tilly—yes, we're at the *Call me Tilly* phase of our relationship.

"Good." I shrug. I know I should tell her about Leon. But I also know that she would want to go down a whole rabbit hole about how he and I know each other, how I felt about him back then, what motivated me to fall into bed with him, and why I'm not interested in pursuing anything more serious, with him or anyone.

I'm too raw for that at this point, with the endorphins from last night still coursing through my body. Plus, it really was a hookup. She doesn't need to know about every random sexcapade.

So instead I say, "It's weird to be back here. I don't know, not bad exactly. But I'm still feeling really frustrated about job stuff. I spent the morning working on it, and that just made me feel more defeated." Tilly is basically the only person who knows I'm lucky I was given this time away instead of straight-up getting fired.

"What do you mean, 'working on it'?"

"I made a list of jobs."

"What's on it?"

"No, not like, jobs for me. Just . . . occupations."

"You're halfway to a Richard Scarry book." Tilly stifles a laugh, and I grin back at her, despite myself. "But also, Cassidy, I want you to consider that maybe you don't need to have a plan right now. Maybe you can take this time in California to really be *off* and just unwind and recover for a little while."

Oh, that bit again. She said it when I first told her about all of this too. I know she's probably right in theory, but I can't imagine how I could possibly *do nothing* for more than an hour at a time. I've never been a go-with-the-flow person. Getting stuff done is my love language. Basically my religion.

"Relaxing is not in my nature," I respond a little petulantly.

"Can you think of the last time you tried it?" she shoots back. The problem with having seen the same therapist for this long is that I'm way past the bullshit stage. Tilly knows exactly how—and when—to call me on mine.

She cocks her head. "I know not working reminds you of a hard time in your life," she continues, much more gently. "But twenty-eight is not twenty-two, and you aren't who you were then either. It might be okay to loosen your grip a little bit."

When she says it like that, it sounds simple. Like they always say in yoga classes, *Surrender! Let go!* But that would involve examining my body to see which muscles are tense. And then acknowledging that it's all of them.

And that's before we even get to what's going on in my head.

I change the subject to my parents and their trip, and Tilly lets me, though we both know it's filler. She also knows me well enough to know when the pushing stops being productive.

After we sign off, I look at my phone and see that I have two texts. One is from Willa, confirming that we're still on for drinks tonight. The other is from Maya.

Maya and I aren't exactly close, but we've stayed in touch over the years, and there's an unspoken intimacy between us. Less in a *We've fucked the same guy* kind of way and more in a *Our names will forever be linked to the same misogyny-laden national scandal* kind of way. I run into her at fundraisers sometimes, and we've been able to confide in each other when Cooper's in the news again, as he was during President Knight's reelection campaign two years ago. And again now that he's about to get remarried in September.

According to the tabloid coverage that finds me whether I like it or not, his fiancée is a New York socialite a decade younger than him. She's from a family whose money is even older than *his* family's political dynasty, and they seem to be nauseatingly well matched: gorgeous surfaces who exist mostly to reflect the light just so. Maya is usually too diplomatic to talk shit, especially when the subject is a major political donor. But when the news of their engagement broke, she described Kit Randolph to me as "decorative and hollow as a gourd."

I slide open the message from her: *Heads-up: Coop has a feature in* GQ *about becoming a new man. Apparently he had a near-death experience while sailing last year.*

I laugh out loud. Typical. I write back, *Thanks for the warning. It's giving the* Odyssey*?*

She replies with a skull emoji. Then: *How are you doing?*

It's not her fault that the answer to that question is a minefield. And of all the people I'm not about to take my problems to, Maya McPherson tops the list. So I settle for something that's true but not revealing: *I'm surviving.*

I know the feeling comes back a few minutes later. And then, *Take care of yourself, Cassidy.*

Whatever tightened in my jaw at the sight of Cooper's name relaxes just a little bit. I have been lucky in a lot of ways—by the time my sex scandal broke, at least some people had learned their lesson about shaming very young women for getting involved with older, powerful men. I always had defenders, even if they were sometimes hard to hear over the shouts of people suggesting I kill myself. But it was hard to take any of them seriously until I had Maya's forgiveness. And I never take that for granted.

You too, I send back.

The texts from her are a welcome reminder to get over myself. I've been fortunate in too many ways, supported by too many people, to sit around moping.

I remember something that a career counselor said to me at some point during my postscandal purgatory. He advised me to start my job search not with titles or industries but instead with my values. To think about what I liked and wanted generally before I got too specific. So I open a new Google Doc and start a new list: *Things I Like*.

This is somewhere between working and relaxing, I tell myself as I type out phrases like *Talking to people* and *Making connections* and *Having a flexible schedule*. It almost feels stupid. Who doesn't like that stuff? But as my fingers move, my brain calms, and the thoughts come faster and clearer. *Finding meaning in what I do. Forming real relationships. Working with vulnerable people. Learning on the job.*

By the time I have to leave to meet Willa, I have a messy, incomplete, and imperfect rundown of what matters to me. It's not as much as I want, but at least it's a start.

V

I show up for our drinks date five minutes early, and at first, I'm not sure I'm in the right space.

Willa's been a talented artist since we met in elementary school, but a few years ago, her career really took off. She started selling her ceramics on TikTok as a side hustle, her customer base grew steadily, and then, bam, Goop put one of her serving platters in their gift guide, and she sold out of everything on her site instantly.

She's spent the last eight months scrambling to catch up with demand; now she's opening a bona fide storefront / community space: Somewhere she can sell her own stuff and also host pottery workshops and parties and feature other artists' work.

Or at least that's how she described it to me over text. When I first moved away for college, we used to FaceTime weekly, but over the years, that's evolved into random texts and voice notes and rare moments of serendipity when we're both free at the same time so that those exchanges can take the shape of a conversation. Luckily we've always maintained the same sense of closeness and ease—an ability to pick back up where we left off.

When she told me her shop would be on Fourth Street, I pictured the sleek retail section that's sprung up in the last decade: near the Warby Parker store, maybe, across from the Aesop. Instead, I'm six blocks away, in front of what looks like a barely converted warehouse. The only real sign of life is that the front door has been freshly painted a bright geranium red.

I knock and then wait. And wait. And wait. After a couple minutes, I'm about to call when the door bursts open, and there she is: Willa Daniels, in all of her glory. Her hair is barely restrained by a bandanna. Her brown skin is clear like she's never had a zit—which she hasn't, at least on my watch. She's covered in a fine layer of what I think is sawdust and flecked all over with clay. She looks great—she always looks great—but her dark-brown eyes have circles underneath them.

A goofy smile breaks across her face when she sees me. She opens her arms for a hug. "I can't believe you're really here! How long were you knocking? I was just in the back and didn't hear you; I really lost track of time. Someone from *Elle* was here earlier—did I tell you they're doing a profile?—which is so cool, but I thought the interview was going to be thirty minutes, and it ran two hours, and my day just got kind of . . . fucked."

She's always bubbly, but she also sounds a little frenetic. Frantic, even. "Should we reschedule?" I offer. "If you're too tired . . ."

Willa looks at me like I'm being crazy. "Oh my god, no, we have to get drinks. I've been here for like twenty-four hours straight at this point, and I don't think—I'm not sure I had lunch?" She looks like she genuinely doesn't remember, which is distressing. "Also, I'm not gonna let you leave Berkeley before we've fully, properly caught up. I did the math, and it's two fucking years since the last time we saw each other in person."

I flinch. I haven't been *avoiding* my hometown per se, but there haven't been many occasions that have demanded my presence, and I haven't made it my business to do anything about that. Most holiday celebrations happen with extended family in Philly, so I've had a whole litany of excuses to keep me on the other coast. It might be closer to four years since I've been back, but I'm not gonna remind Willa of that. "Too long," I say and squeeze her forearm. "Wanna give me a quick tour before we leave, or will that just stress you out more?"

"No, no, come inside. Just watch your step—I had my sister here earlier to help paint, and she brought her kids, so I can't guarantee there aren't still stray monster trucks lying around."

She turns and waves me inside. "The space was completely raw when we signed the lease. Bryce"—Willa's boyfriend—"refinished the floors himself and installed all of the tile in the bathrooms. It's really been so crazy, Cass. I learned how to caulk? And install dimmers? But it is amazing to be able to make the space exactly how I want it to be."

I follow behind her, taking it all in. I'm equal parts proud and jealous, and my instinct to hide from both feelings kicks in. I can see why she fell in love with the space, even though it's still kind of a mess. Overhead skylights make up for the lack of front windows, and the early evening sun streams onto the wooden planks under my feet.

But I can also see uneven patches and drips where her nephews probably distracted her makeshift painting crew. There's no furniture yet or lighting fixtures. In one corner of the ceiling, there's a cluster of dangling wires that looks potentially life-threatening. She has two and a half weeks until opening, twenty days to make enough inventory to stock the store and also make the space look like . . . a store. I have a feeling she's going to need every one of them.

"Is it just you and whatever family members you can rustle up to help you?" I ask.

"Bryce is here on weekends, but his job's hellish during the week," Willa says. "Some friends come in when they can. And, actually, I hired someone. He's been a huge help."

"That's so fancy!"

"Oh, it's not that fancy."

"It is to me! An employee!"

She smiles fondly. "He barely listens to me."

"No. You're the boss! Is he a CCA student? An arty local? Where did you find him?"

Willa looks more amused by this conversation than she should. "You can come see for yourself," she says. "Then we'll go."

She gestures to a door propped open along the back wall, and as I step across the threshold, I mostly see more chaos.

The floor is covered in bags of clay, boxes of brushes, and glaze chemicals. Half of the tables hold pieces in progress covered by loose plastic sheeting. A central workspace is laid out with more boxes plus tools and notebooks. One corner holds the kiln; across the room from it is a pottery wheel. Willa became known for her hand-pinched pieces but has started to throw more lately, in part to keep up with demand.

There's a person angled over the wheel. His dark head is bent in concentration, and long, nimble fingers carefully shape a mound of wet clay. He's wearing a cutoff tank top, and his arms flex as he gently urges the material out and up to make the beginning of what looks like a cup. A tattoo winds up one forearm, across his biceps.

A tattoo I know. A tattoo I had to resist the urge to lick last night.

"Hey, Lee. Look who's here," Willa calls out, a little too much honey in her voice.

He looks up, and for the second time in twenty-four hours, I find myself unexpectedly face-to-face with Leon Park.

Of course. Of course this is happening. Willa never did understand why I hated Leon so much; they stayed friends even after she and Zeke broke up. And he would be the kind of guy who would be up for helping Willa out with this job, as long as she's lenient with his hours, depending on the surf report.

You just put "flexible schedule" on your list of future job requirements, the voice in my head starts before I tell it to shut the fuck up. Then Leon shakes his hair out of his face, and I realize that the specks I saw last night weren't paint—they were bits of dried glaze. I would ask what I'm being punished for if the answer wasn't so obvious.

The pottery wheel is still turning in brisk, even circles, but Leon's hand clenches, and the vessel he was shaping collapses beneath it. He looks down at the mess and scowls. "Well that's done," he says. He stands up and wipes his palms on his jeans. My eyes linger on the wet patches on his thighs.

The feeling of being caught off guard makes me feisty. "Hi, Leon," I say too brightly.

"Hi." He turns his back to me as he goes to the sink to rinse his hands. Then he turns around again and regards me coolly. "What are you doing here?"

It's impossible not to feel glaringly self-conscious. Does he already regret what happened last night? Or worse, does he think I showed up here, like, to see him?

I try desperately to figure out how to convey that I'm as shocked by this turn of events as he is. "Does Leon really *work for you*?" I ask Willa in a thin, demanding tone. I wince as I see how it lands.

He narrows his eyes and answers before she can. "Sorry, is that too plebeian for you, Cassidy?"

I instantly feel like shit. If I had any fantasies that one night of spectacular sex would change the tenor of things between us, they've been thoroughly shattered. We haven't been in each other's presence for five minutes, and we're back to the status quo: feints and jabs. Polite smiles doing nothing to mask irritation and aggression.

Willa looks back and forth between us and sighs. "This is why I didn't warn either of you about this. I was hoping that you could just . . . be normal about each other for once. Clearly too much to ask. But yes, Cassidy, Leon works with me. Leon, Cassidy and I are about to take off to get a drink. Two more minutes, and then you can go back to ignoring each other for the rest of eternity. Okay?"

"Fine with me," Leon grumbles.

"Me too," I say.

Willa rolls her eyes. Then, to Leon, she says, "See you tomorrow?"

"Tomorrow's the—" He gestures with one hand.

"Oh right, the cabinetry gig. That's fine. I'll manage."

Leon nods and goes back to the wheel. Willa grabs her purse off a chair and turns to me. "Let's go?"

Judging by the way the bartender greets Willa at the bar a few blocks from the shop, she's already a regular.

I grimace at the sight of a martini on the cocktail menu and opt for a glass of pinot noir. Do like the locals do. When we settle ourselves into a velvet-lined booth, I consider telling Willa about last night with Leon—ten years ago, it would already have been out of my mouth—but then Willa leans her head back and sighs deeply. She really does look tired.

"For real, how are you holding up?" I ask.

Willa keeps her eyes closed. "Fine."

"Okay, but I gotta tell you, you're not being very convincing."

She opens her eyelids, lolls her head toward me, and smiles. "You just caught me at the end of a long day. And Leon being out tomorrow—it's going to make things harder. That's all."

"He has another job?" I venture in the most neutral tone I can muster. It's the natural next question, is all.

"I mean, I can't pay him much. That he's working for me is practically a favor at this point, and I'd be completely screwed without him. I gave him some equity in the business, so if we're ever profitable, he'll have a stake. But for now, he's still picking up carpentry jobs to make ends meet."

I nod, but internally I steel myself against even the idea of giving him any credit. I appreciate that Leon is doing Willa a solid, but if I know him, soon enough, he'll be on to the next, and it's likely to leave Willa in a pinch.

"What do you have to do tomorrow?" I ask.

"Painting. That's the first thing, getting those walls finished. They were supposed to be done today, but obviously they're not yet, and until the paint dries, Leon can't install the shelves. Once they're in it'll help me figure out where the pedestals are going to go—but those have to be painted too. Fuck, I forgot about that. And that's not even getting into the electrical stuff, which Leon swears he can do himself, but he's not licensed, and I can't have someone getting electrocuted in my space, you know? So I've got a guy coming, but it's going to be a few days, and—anyway. Sorry. I didn't mean to give you my entire to-do list."

I nudge her with an elbow. "I came to hear how you're doing, so if that's how you're doing, then that's what I'm here for."

Willa fluffs her hair and gives me a smirk. "It's all very glamorous, as you can see."

"It is! I mean, you're a working artist! How many people can say that?"

Willa lets out a long sigh. "I know, I know. I am trying to keep sight of that. I'm definitely working. And I know you get the intensity."

"I do. Which is why I'm actually on sabbatical right now. It felt like too much to get into over text, but I needed a break." I say it with my usual practiced smile-and-laugh, like I'm humble-bragging about a windfall of PTO. There would have been a time when Willa would have seen right through my act, but I've been away for long enough that she doesn't—or if she does, she doesn't say so. My stomach squirms with discomfort. I feel like an asshole, lying to her so baldly. Somehow, it's even worse that she's not questioning it.

"Oh, wow! What are your plans?" she asks.

"You know, I don't really . . . have any."

As I admit it, an idea takes shape in my mind. It's obviously a bad one. It would involve doing exactly what Tilly told me to avoid. And probably bring me back into contact with Leon.

But, the excuse-making part of my brain reasons, *she just said Leon won't be there tomorrow. And if you help for one day—that's not a big deal, is it? You can rest for two and a half weeks after that.*

"What if I came in to help tomorrow?" I blurt before I can talk myself out of it.

Willa's face lights up. "Oh my god, really? That would be amazing, Cass. I can't pay you, but I'd buy you lunch or something. I have a bunch of inventory that all needs to get priced and input into the SKU system, and if you could help me with the painting and then do that for even just an hour—or two—"

I laugh. "You have me all day."

VI

The next morning, Willa greets me with a bag of donuts and coffee, and we eat standing up, scattering crumbs on the newspapers she laid down before I got there. "Shit. This is good," I mumble around a mouthful.

"It's, like, a yeasted dough or something?"

"I can't remember the last time I had a donut." I search the bag for a napkin. "Breakfast in general. My mornings are usually a rush to the door."

Willa frowns, and I mentally kick myself for broaching the subject. "Too busy for hoovering up a pastry? You might need a new job."

I take a big bite to avoid having to answer her right away. I managed to sidestep this topic pretty handily last night, and I could brush her off now. But that feeling in my stomach—the one I got from lying to her—hasn't gone away. Willa used to be the person I told everything: what it felt like to have sex for the first time, that I was scared to move to DC for college despite my bravado. Realizing that we've grown this far apart—that I don't even know how to open up to *her* anymore—makes me feel like an alien to myself in a way I don't like.

I nudge at some crumbs with the toe of my sneaker. I try to make my voice extremely casual when I say, "Yeah, actually, I've been thinking that maybe I do. It might be time to try something new." Not the full truth, but closer to it than I've gotten with anyone else.

Willa dusts her hands off and grabs a paint roller from a bucket. "Kim Miller is opening up a med spa in Nob Hill," she says. "How do you feel about supporting rich women on their youth-preservation journeys?"

I crinkle my nose. "I feel like you're just looking for an excuse to show me a current photo of Kim Miller."

Willa shrugs with a coy smile.

"I mean, good for her, but if there's one thing I've learned from dealing with our donors, it's that whatever I do next, I'd like to be further removed from the ultrarich."

"She offered to do my elevens last time I saw her. I'm still considering it." Willa waggles her brows.

"When was that?"

"Just a couple of months ago. Our ten-year reunion."

Our high school doesn't have my email address, and Willa knows better than to bother inviting me to those sorts of things. "How was that?"

Willa paints a corner as she considers her answer. She has strong arms and a steady hand. "It was kind of fun, actually. Just to see everyone and realize how much we've all changed."

"Leon—" I start before I realize that I'm about to divulge too much information. *Leon said Zeke has a kid now*, I was going to say. But Willa heard every word of our conversation yesterday, and she knows perfectly well that wasn't part of it. Looks like I've encountered the limits of my ambitions to open up. "Leon doesn't seem that different," I correct myself hastily.

Willa rolls her eyes. "Cassidy, for real?"

"What?"

"You saw him for ten minutes. You have no idea what he's like. And at this point, I thought you of all people wouldn't be so judgmental."

My face heats, and there's an awkward silence. Do I wish being publicly humiliated turned me into a saint? Sure. But turns out I'm still capable of being just as uncharitable with everyone as I've always been.

"You know me," I say when I think I can get my voice to behave. "Never learned a lesson in my life."

"Sorry," she says immediately. "I wasn't being fair."

"No, you were. I'm definitely the biggest screw-up in our grade. Leon doesn't even come close." I dunk my roller in the paint tray with too much gusto.

"Okay, yeah, no. That's definitely not my point at all." A lot of people are too intimidated by me—my pain, my scandal—to touch it. But Willa puts her roller down and comes over to wrap her arms around me. "I love you," she says. "And I love Leon. And I wish you could see each other the way I see each of you. That's all I meant."

I lean my head on her shoulder. She's wearing a new

perfume these days; she doesn't smell like Marc Jacobs Daisy anymore. But she's still familiar in the most important ways. "I love you too."

She gives me a squeeze and lets me go. "You two have always been square waves."

I have no idea what that means.

"Still not an ocean person—why do I find that comforting? They're two dueling waves that make for bad conditions. For everyone." She points to herself.

"Okay, so paint me a picture." I focus on the wall, on actual paint. "Tell me about the Leon you know."

She nods. "He's curious. Like, when the kiln stopped working a few weeks ago, I just hired someone to come fix it. But Leon spent the whole afternoon with him. Learning what had gone wrong and what else could go wrong with kilns like ours. He wanted to understand more about it."

I nod. Roll up, roll down. Up, down.

"And he's learned how not to be such a perfectionist. He tries stuff, even if he thinks he might be bad at it."

I can't help myself; I make a little scoffing noise.

"What now?"

"I just . . . that's not how I remember him. As like, striving for *perfection*."

Willa pauses to check her phone. Her lock screen is dense with notifications, and she triages for a minute before turning back to me.

"Not to overshare on his behalf, but it's something he and I have talked about a lot. And the way he describes it, he would get, like, paralyzed by how badly he wanted to be good at stuff. So instead of trying at all, he just wouldn't. It made him crazy, being that hard on himself. We were talking about the senior art show the other day, and . . ." She trails off with a chuckle. I sigh. It's been so long since I thought about *Procrastination*.

All through high school, I was in student government, and senior year, I was the events chair. With Willa's help, I pulled together a gallery show that paired student work with local artists' pieces. It ended up being a notably successful fundraiser that paid for new band uniforms.

I'd been surprised when Leon signed up to participate. I knew he'd been in Willa's studio art class sophomore year, but I didn't realize he had been that into it.

In the weeks leading up to it, he refused to describe his piece to me. I needed to know if I was supposed to hang it or put it on a stand, if it was a drawing or a painting or a sculpture and how big or small. What the theme was, so I could group similar work together. But I got . . . nothing. So I ended up reserving a whole corner of the room for him, just in case. When the day arrived, he handed me an index card. It said, *Procrastination: An Ongoing Performance by Leon Park*.

Boiling over with anger, I stuck it up on the wall with blue painter's tape. And of course, it was a hit. All night I had to watch people read it and laugh and congratulate him. While I fielded complaints from visitors who were annoyed that one of the bathrooms was out of order.

I think about what I said to him the other night: *People*

like boys who fail way better than girls who succeed. With *Procrastination*, it felt so clear that everyone loved him for his effortlessness in a way they'd never love me for all of my effort. I had disliked him before, but that was when I truly started to detest him.

So despite the explanation Willa's offering me, it's hard for me to conjure much sympathy or understanding. "Let's talk about something else," I say. "Like your birthday party. I'm very excited to meet Bryce."

"And he's excited to meet you." Willa stands back to consider our progress so far. "And for you to see our house. I've obviously been a wreck since we moved in, but he's done a sort of miraculous job getting everything set up. It turns out he's kind of a genius interior designer?"

If I didn't love Willa so much, I might hate her too. It's hard not to feel like she has the life we're supposed to have at our age: a sweet, caring partner; a cool job that she created for herself; and a *house*, instead of some tiny one-bedroom apartment she can barely afford. I can still see my high school best friend when I look at her, but she's grown into herself so much too. I'm not sure that I've done the same.

"I think Ellery is coming too. And Dana, and Izzy—half of our old study hall crew, basically." Willa laughs. "And you'll really like Bryce's work friends—they're nonprofit people too. Actually, one or two are hot and single."

Maybe if I have another fling, it'll wash the taste of Leon out of my mouth. "Well, I'll make sure to wear something cute then."

"Bonus points if it's what you wore to my eighteenth

birthday," she says with a wink. Oh god, the sequin mini-dress. Before I can remind her about what *she* wore to that particular event, Willa's focus shifts back to what's on the wall. "Okay, sorry, but can you go over that last section again? It's looking a little uneven."

We paint for another couple of hours, long enough that by the time we're done, my forearms, shoulders, and back are all aching. We keep talking, the kind of rambling conversation you can only have when you have a long afternoon together. One that makes me realize how much I've missed Willa. One that makes the morning fly by so much faster than it did when I was on my laptop yesterday.

I feel . . . useful. It's a novel sensation, and I don't want to give it up. I know what Tilly said yesterday, but right now it's hard not to feel like, *Fuck that, actually*. I don't need more time alone with my thoughts. I know them, they're exhausting, and I'm tired of hanging out with them.

And then there's the feeling I get when Willa gives me a hug goodbye in the late afternoon. The rest of my day flashes before me: the quiet of my parents' house. Going for a solo walk. Having a lonely dinner. It makes me feel like I'm staring down a long, dark tunnel. It's a panic I recognize. And one I can't bear.

I blurt out, "Do you want me to come back tomorrow?"

Willa narrows her eyes. "Leon will be back tomorrow."

"No, I know, and I don't want to be in the way. It's just

that I was thinking—I am on this break. So I have all of this free time, and I kind of don't know what to do with it. And it seems like maybe—"

She waves a hand at me like she's swatting a fly. "I need *so* much help." Her hands move to her hips. "But I don't want to be in the middle of a Cassidy and Leon grudgefest for the next two weeks. I'm tired enough as it is."

"I know. I promise—I can be cool."

She gives me a skeptical look. One I've definitely earned. But then she sighs and nods. "Okay. Can you be here by ten?"

VII

Willa must have talked to Leon about our deal, because when I stroll into the store the next morning—wearing a coat of mascara and a lip stain, so sue me—he barely looks up from hanging shelving.

So I get to work.

We spend our days avoiding each other. It's actually not that hard—he's assigned to big projects that involve technical expertise and difficult manual labor, and I'm more of a glorified errand runner. I paint walls, I pick up coffees and lunches, I input SKUs into the inventory system. If we end up in the same room, Leon and I nod briskly and say as little as possible to each other. "Is there any more coffee?" from me. "Can you grab the door?" from him.

But that doesn't keep me from noticing just how good he is at what he does. Willa was right that he's inquisitive, and it's evident he's put his curiosity to good use, teaching himself how to do a little bit of almost everything. When the electrician does finally show up, two days delayed, he and Leon talk technicalities that make my head spin. Leon's the only person aside from Willa who's allowed to touch the temperamental kiln. He lugs bags of clay from one place to another, and his lean arms flex with hard muscle when he does. I learn more than I should about the way the curves of his tattoo shift when he moves. The focused expression he makes when he takes product photography and determines pedestal placement.

By the time the end of the week rolls around, I'm a ball of prickly frustration. I've been helpful, but I haven't revealed myself to be particularly talented at anything—no secret skill, no path to a lifelong career. That, and I'm annoyed that I can't stop thinking about how, even though he's an asshole who hates me, I still want Leon Park.

And now I'm also stuck with the knowledge that if I were to give in to temptation again, the sex would be incredible.

Friday's weather exacerbates my desire to crawl out of my own skin. It's a rare hot day, and there's no AC in the space, so everything feels stuffy and sticky. Willa has a meeting with a potential collector in the afternoon—a fancy art guy—so she's extra-anxious herself.

She spends the morning fussing over everything, changing her mind so many times that finally, Leon tells her she needs to chill, which means that she comes to vent to me. It's not yet 11 a.m., and everyone's nervy and sweaty, and the air feels charged.

Willa leaves, but that tension remains. Leon is doing

something in the back room, and he's playing music too loudly for me to concentrate. I put on headphones. He sees me, and I swear to god he turns the music up louder. In retaliation, I go out for coffee and a chocolate croissant and don't get him anything, which is particularly rude because it's impossible to spend a day here without learning how obsessed that boy is with a good pastry.

By 2 p.m., I'm dying to get out and go for a walk. I packed a sandwich that's sitting in the refrigerator, but I decide I'm allowed to ignore it and take myself out, if only for a change of scenery.

But as I'm about to leave, there's a knock on the front door. I open it to a heavily perspiring delivery man. "Hey," he says brusquely. "Where do you want it?"

"Want . . . what?"

"All of this."

He gestures behind him, and I see what he's talking about: a dolly loaded with extremely large boxes labeled HEAVY and also FRAGILE.

Oh Jesus fucking Christ. This is the last thing I need right now. My stomach is growling, the air is stifling, and I have no idea what's in those packages, much less where they're supposed to go.

I don't want to ask Leon. But also I know calling Willa in the middle of her big meeting is not an option.

I take a deep breath and then release it. "Can you hang on a sec?"

"Sure, but if you could make it quick—I'm running late, and I need to get going."

SQUARE WAVES

"Of course, of course, just let me—" I hurry across the room and open the door to the back, sticking my head through. "Leon, are we expecting a delivery?"

He jumps at the sound of my voice. He's been sitting at the table in the back, sketching while eating, and one of his hands goes to cover whatever he's been drawing. "No."

"Okay, I just, there's a guy here, with a dolly?"

Leon's face changes in an instant, and he's on his feet. "Oh fuck, is this the Villeneuve delivery?"

"I don't know, he didn't—"

Leon is already striding past me.

But at the door, the delivery man has already unloaded the shipment. So much for *Where do you want these?* "Can you sign, please?" he asks, holding out his clipboard.

Leon dashes off a signature. And then it's just me and him and the boxes. There are ten of them, three or four feet on each side. HEAVY and FRAGILE start to look like taunts.

Leon sighs. He wipes his forehead, damp already from the heat. "We need to get these to the far corner." Then, with a withering look at me, "I can probably do it myself."

I shrug, taking some comfort in the well-worn groove of our mutual distaste, grab my bag, and head for the door. Then I make a crucial mistake. I glance over at Leon and see how hard he's struggling. The boxes are a little too wide for his wingspan, and they're too unbalanced for him to carry. He curses, steps back. Considers his options.

I picture Willa's disappointed face if something were to get damaged just because I felt the need to prove a point.

Then Leon attempts another lift. It seems like it's going better, but then the box shifts, starts to slip, and I can't help it: I drop my bag on the floor and dash over before it falls out of his hands. Our eyes meet, and we almost smile.

"Thanks," Leon says.

"Yeah, well. These look expensive. Too many loud warning stickers on the packages for them not to be."

Leon laughs. It's the first time I've seen his face open up since—

Not useful.

"What's in these, anyway?" I ask as we both try to strategically position ourselves around the corners of cardboard.

"Do you know who Alan Villeneuve is?"

"Nope."

"He's a glassworker. Makes these chandeliers that— actually, once we move them, I'll open one up and show you. They're pretty amazing."

"Okay." The tension between us lessens by a couple of degrees. "So should we just . . . walk?"

"I think we should try it."

We do a kind of shimmy, each of us grasping the short ends of the box. My hands are sweaty and my fingers are cramping by the time we gently—so gently—lower it back to the floor.

"One down." I wipe my palms on my cutoff shorts.

Leon takes a beat too long to respond. "And nine to go."

I roll my wrists. "How did you get so in-the-know about the art world?" I'm proud that I don't sound as accusatory as I usually do with him.

Leon nods. "I worked at a coffee shop in college, and one of my coworkers was a really great sculptor. That's the funny thing about the odd-job life—it's either burnouts or superfocused side hustlers. Anyway, she introduced me to a lot of cool people. And their work started to change my perspective on it."

A flare of jealousy burns in my stomach, which is completely ridiculous. I know literally nothing about this woman, except that she . . . exists. And Leon thinks she's cool. Which, so what?

"Were you—back there—I didn't mean to snoop, but—"

"I was sketching something for a painting I'm making." Leon looks at his feet before lifting his eyes to mine, seemingly with some effort. "Willa asked me to hang some pieces here."

I think of *Procrastination*—of course I do—but I don't consider bringing it up. Progress. "Oh. That's cool."

"Yeah. It is."

Leon nods to me, and we pick up the second box in silent tandem.

"So what do you think of this Rick guy?" I ask as we start to move. "The one Willa's having lunch with?"

"Richard," Leon corrects me. "Richard Kerrigan."

"Right. Him."

Leon shakes his head. The movement almost sends him off balance, and he doesn't answer until we've put the box down. "He's legit. He used to be one of the most famous art dealers in San Francisco. He retired to Marin a few years ago, but then he got bored. He's not officially in the business anymore, but he buys and sells out of his home sometimes, and being part of his personal collection is the ultimate. He's gotten more into functional art recently—furniture, glassware, pottery. The kind of stuff Willa does. His house is, like, a thing."

By the time we return for the third one, we've found our rhythm with the boxes. When we're done, I'm covered in a film of sweat, and so is Leon. He's wearing a perfect Bay Area skater outfit today: a pair of khaki Dickies, a T-shirt so worn-in that it's practically translucent. He lifts the hem to wipe his face, and I'm hit by a wave of memory: what it felt like to linger there. To dip my head lower, and taste him. The room smells like him, that same intoxicating mix of exertion and Old Spice, and I'm terrified that he can see it on my face.

Maybe that's why I blurt out, "Did you tell anyone what happened?"

Leon's expression goes wary in an instant. "What?"

Nice to know I'm the only one still thinking about it. But it's too late to back down, so I say, "You know. About us. What happened the other night."

"No." His eyes narrow as he assesses me. Then he turns toward the first box we moved. He crouches down, pulls a box cutter out of his pocket, and runs it along one of the carefully taped seams.

"Aren't you going to ask me if I told anyone?"

"No."

"Why not?"

"Because, Cassidy." He puts the blade down and stands

back up. He sounds like he's being very patient with me. "I know you. And I know you'd never admit that you lowered yourself to sleeping with *me*."

That he's not wrong just makes me angrier. "But aren't you equally ashamed that you slept with me? That you couldn't resist my try-hard, bitchy wiles?"

"You didn't have to try very hard, as far as I recall."

I cannot *believe* he's using my orgasm against me. All of the resentments I've been storing up for way too long come spilling out. "You know, I never finished answering your question, at the bar. It wasn't just that time in seventh grade. It was every time after that. It was when you slouched into class late and sat in the back and laughed like all of us who were there to take it seriously were some kind of joke to you. It's that the *last* time you made any art, it was nothing more than a wink at your own cleverness, a *fuck you* to me, and a reminder that you can get away with anything if you feel like it. It's the way you *are*, Leon. You act like nothing in the world matters to you. Not school, not girls, certainly not me—"

Leon scoffs. "What was the purpose of me trying to impress you back then, or even now? And when was I supposed to do it, for that matter? When you were making a point of showing me up in school? Or at the bar when you treated me like I was still that same eighteen-year-old? You've made it very clear exactly what you think of me: that I'm a slacker *well* beneath your notice. But look where we both ended up: right fucking here."

In the silence that follows, I realize we've both been

shouting. Leon's breathing hard, like he just ran a mile. Like he's gotten something off his chest that he's been waiting more than a decade to say.

I want to come back at him. To tell him he's wrong, and I'm right and always have been. But when he puts it that way—I don't know. I don't like the version of me he's describing either.

My hand throbs with a cramp, and I realize I've clenched it into a reflexive fist. The muscles protest as I force it to uncurl. *God*, I think. I've been defending myself against Leon's imagined dislike for so long that I never really thought about how it was for him to be on the receiving end of my anger.

Once I've had that thought, all of the fight goes out of me. I pull my hair off my neck and huff out a breath, like it's the temperature and the work that's doing this to me, not him. At least one thing is clear: I need to get out of here, *now*.

"I'm gonna go get some lunch," I say.

"Whatever."

I grab my bag from where I dropped it. Behind me, I can hear Leon opening the seam of the next box, and I remember his offer to show me what was in them. I am curious, but I don't dare turn back.

Instead, I release myself into the heat of the day.

When I return, the charge of the space has dissipated, and Leon is holed up in the back. But he did unpack the boxes, and their contents are on display: a series of intricate glass mobiles, each of them rainbow-hued and shimmering in the sun streaming through the skylights. They throw rainbows onto the walls and puddles of color onto the floors.

My eyes go wet. I can't remember the last time I saw anything so beautiful. I want to ask about them—how they're made. What they mean. If he got emotional at the sight of them too.

But that would mean having to acknowledge everything we just yelled at each other. The rage we've been sitting on for stupidly long. So instead, I go back to the table and open the laptop. My ears perk at any sound coming from the back, but I don't see him for the rest of the day.

VIII

When I get home that evening, I take a long shower. I try to let everything drain out of my body: residual anger, which is quickly being replaced by a rising tide of shame. I really did always think that Leon couldn't be bothered to care what I said or thought about him. That I couldn't hurt him the way he hurt me.

I remember what Willa said about him the other day—that he was a perfectionist, and that's why he never finished anything. At the time it was easy to brush off. I'm *a perfectionist*, I thought. *That's why I work so hard to get things accomplished*.

But against my will, I start to see what she meant. And I can imagine being sixteen and seventeen and scared and embarrassed, in part because I've been twenty-two and scared and embarrassed. The way that his lazy stoner thing was as much of a pose then as my *Don't worry, I have it all together* thing is now.

Which means I probably owe him an apology or something. I'm grateful to be able to put it off until Monday, at least. Tonight is Willa's birthday party, but I overheard him telling her he couldn't make it—one of his sisters is doing an open mic tonight, and he can't miss it.

I lean into getting ready in a way I sometimes do when I need to declutter my head. I blow-dry my hair until it's soft and sleek. I do my regular makeup, add a flick of eyeliner, and pull out the dress I've been planning on wearing all week. It's a billowy high-neck minidress that shows off my legs.

When I still thought Leon was coming to the party, I had been enjoying picturing his face seeing me in it. I hoped he would blush. Choke on his drink. Remember exactly how badly he wanted me and know that he couldn't have me again. But now that just seems like more evidence of who he thinks I am: a self-centered brat with a superiority complex. I'm glad I don't have to rethink my wardrobe choices before I head out into the night.

And yet I regret them as soon as I step outside. Even a warm day here cools dramatically as the sun sets, and immediately, my bare legs prick with goose bumps. I lament the outfit choice even more when Bryce opens the door to the house wearing a Henley, jeans, and a garden-worn pair of Blundstones. It's too easy to forget what passes for dressed-up in this city.

My self-imposed Instagram ban means I've only ever seen Bryce in a couple of photos Willa texted, but in person, he's exactly as handsome and charming as I would have guessed. Willa has consistently excellent taste in men. (Unlike some of us.) He welcomes me, tells me that he has no idea where Willa is, and insists on giving me a tour of the house, pointing out the curtains made from deadstock fabric and the vintage couch he scored a deal on through Facebook Marketplace. Willa was right—this place looks great, and he's clearly put a ton of effort into making it that way.

Our last stop is the kitchen, where Bryce uncorks a bottle of wine while I choose a ceramic cup from a spread of them, all presumably made by Willa's hand. "To you saving the birthday girl's ass this week," he says, lifting his drink.

"Honestly, she's saving my ass. I don't have any other plans while I'm here. I'd be climbing the walls if she didn't give me something to do."

"Tell me about it. Willa is always making fun of me for how many hobbies I have, but what's wrong with liking to stay busy?"

"Yes!" I'm more emphatic than I need to be, but I feel affirmed. *See?* I want to tell Tilly. *Not wanting to do nothing is hardly pathological.*

When the front door swings open again, Bryce takes off to attend to his host duties, and I'm left to my own devices.

I've gotten over the worst of the social anxiety that being at the center of a public scandal gave me, but sometimes, it rears its head again. Especially when I'm by myself at parties. I worry that everyone is noticing that I'm alone—and then that they're noticing me, period. Wondering *Why do I know her?* and *Why is she here?* and *Who does she think she is?* and *Why the fuck does she—*

My breathing is already starting to pick up as I slink from the kitchen into the living room.

SQUARE WAVES

Thank god Izzy Gregson is there. She and I weren't particularly close in high school—Willa was kind of our only Venn diagram overlap—but we've always gotten along, and I've never been happier to see her than at this moment. I barrel right into her conversation with a guy whose cheekbones could cut glass.

Thankfully, she doesn't seem to mind. "Oh my god, Cassidy!" she crows. "You look amazing. Willa told me you're in town. For how long?"

"Just another couple of weeks."

"And then you're back to DC? You're still there, yeah?"

"Mmmhmm." My stomach lurches at the mention of DC, but I try to ignore it.

Izzy turns to her companion. "Jo, this is Cassidy," she says. "We went to high school together." She directs her attention back to me. "And are you still at that nonprofit?"

I nod. One of the strange things about having a public-facing job—a public-facing life—is that people always remember what I'm up to. While not having social media for the same reasons means I'm mostly in the dark about them.

"I thought I recognized you." Jo shakes my hand. He's a couple of inches shorter than I am, and his eyes are a deep, almost navy blue. "You're very brave."

Any chance of developing a crush on this guy immediately deflates. The self-consciousness I was just shaking off returns in full force. I've never figured out the right response to either of those statements, even though I hear them all the time. Is it *Well, I don't recognize you. And I'm not actually brave, I just did something selfish, and then I was broke and exhausted and qualified for exactly one job?*

I go with my usual awkward, "Oh. Thanks."

"I actually work for an org that does similar work locally—Rainbow Route."

I smile, now biding my time until we can change topics. For me, discussing work involves talking about the worst mistakes I've ever made. Not exactly something I want to do on a weekend night out.

"I'd noticed you weren't doing as many appearances lately, actually," he continues. "Maybe it's weird to say this, but I hope you're . . . okay." Jo shrugs and looks away, and I feel a spark of recognition, the little flicker that alerts me that I'm probably talking to one of my own. It's not a particularly far leap—people don't tend to randomly land in this line of work. But it's also just something I can sense, at this point. Who's ended up under a spotlight, naked and vulnerable, and who hasn't yet had the pleasure.

That changes things for me, and without quite meaning to, I slip into ambassador mode. It's like developing a split consciousness. One part of me is saying, "Oh yeah, I'm okay. Just—the work is so personal. It can be hard to do for long periods of time," and nodding when Jo says, "Yeah, I—I got into it after I transitioned."

The rest of me is retreating into a shell, curling up, exhausted by the constancy of meeting people who already know about the softest parts of me.

It's a privilege, the intimacies they offer me in return. But I'm also *so fucking tired.*

Izzy slings an arm around Jo's shoulders. "Jo's doing incredible work with trans teens," she tells me. "He ran a summer camp last year, and I did some of the social media for it. Talking to those kids—it was so amazing, how much more confident they were on day fourteen than they had been on day one."

"Oh, that's so cool. It must have been wild, figuring out how to organize it. Cabins and food and activities and everything."

That puts Jo at ease; his face breaks into a grin, and he starts telling me about the camp he went to when he was a kid and how he convinced the director to come out of retirement to help him do the first year of Camp Trans. He regales us with tales of being codirector–turned–dessert chef and learning to make cookies for a hundred, instead of ten.

Izzy peppers in her own camp memories and does a reprise of her bunk's theme song to a round of applause from Jo. The two of them seem close in a way that makes me wonder if there's something more between them, or if there could be. I hope so; *someone* should be appreciating this man's face up close and personal, even if it isn't going to be me.

The nostalgia is just winding down when Willa descends on our little group, wrapping me up in a huge hug. She had a good day today, and it shows: When she got back from her meeting, it was with news that Richard Kerrigan is interested in her work, if not fully committed.

"Where did you disappear to?" Izzy demands. "I saw you earlier, and then—"

"Had to take a work call," Willa says, brushing it off like it's nothing. She's in a low-backed jumpsuit and platform heels, and I feel a pang of gratitude that she's as extra as I am.

"At 8 p.m.? On your birthday?" Izzy is aghast.

"It was from an artist, making sure their work got delivered in okay shape. Thanks for helping with that by the way, Cass. Villeneuve is a genius, but his stuff is an absolute pain to handle. I'm glad Leon didn't have to do it alone."

"Oh, yeah it wasn't really—"

"Oooh, you and Leon are working together," Izzy cuts in. "Do I remember right that you guys were, like, basically rivals?"

I don't know how to answer that, but Willa takes it for me. "To my surprise, they've been decently well-behaved."

"Jesus, Leon Park." Izzy's taking every opportunity to reminisce. "Remember when he and his band played the talent show in tenth grade? I really thought they were gonna get superfamous."

"Cassidy missed that one," Willa says, giving me a little smirk. "She was busy making out with Jasper Frye in a bathroom."

"Oh my god!" Izzy crows. "Jasper? God, Cass, you were such an icon."

I put my hands on my face like I'm pretending to be embarrassed, but in fact, I am legitimately overwhelmed. Too much is hitting me at once. The way Willa and Izzy know me best, of course, is as my high school self: just figuring out she was pretty and excited to enjoy the hell out of it. Throwing myself at everything, hard. At a party, I wasn't afraid to attract attention. In fact, I was usually trying to find it.

But then there's also Jo in this circle: someone I'm just meeting, who already knows so much about me. Who knows an entirely different person than Willa did, or does. He's more familiar with the consequences of my recklessness than anything else.

This is why, if I'm being perfectly honest, I avoid coming back here. Because usually, Before Cassidy is just a memory. A phantom. Here, she's someone people actually knew. And who I have to figure out how to reckon with.

IX

By the time I make it home, it's after midnight. The air has gotten colder, and the wind bites hard against my skin as I jiggle my key in the lock of my parents' front door. It can be a little sticky, and I'm relieved when I feel it turn.

But when I push to open it, it won't budge. I give it a little shove, and then a harder one. And then I realize: There are two locks, a regular one, and a dead bolt. I always throw the dead bolt on when I come in. But tonight, I left out the back door. Which uses its own key. One that I don't have.

Fucking fuck.

I walk through the back gate, just to see if I somehow left that entrance open. Obviously, I didn't.

I lean my forehead against the cool pane of glass there, peering into the dark house. "Let me in," I mumble. "Just... let me in, okay?" It doesn't.

I check my bank balance, and the number is exactly what I knew it would be. I get paid pretty well for a non-profit, but I rarely have much of a cushion. Each dollar has started to feel more meaningful without a sense of how long I'll keep this job and what I'll do next if I don't.

I get a full-body chill as I contemplate just how much I'll shame-spiral if I call a twenty-four-hour locksmith, which will almost certainly run me a few hundred bucks.

Then another idea dawns on me. If it works, it would be far cheaper. Well, except for the cost to my pride and dignity. But I've been known to throw those away for less.

I steel myself, pull out my phone, and text Leon—or the number I assume is his from the group text Willa sent earlier this week. *Hi. Any chance your miseducation has included learning how to pick locks?*

I immediately wish I could unsend it. If he says yes, then I have to move that apology up by forty-eight hours. If he doesn't, I'm out my pride, dignity, *and* however much a professional charges.

I sink down onto the front steps and pull my dress over my knees as best I can while I wait. A few minutes later he writes back, *Are you admitting that you need me for something?*

Beggars can't be choosers. *Yes.*

Your parents still at the same house?

My face warms that he remembers. *They are. Send me your address, and I'll send you an Uber.*

Twenty-five minutes later, Leon's stepping out of the Uber. He's appropriately dressed for the weather, in the same outfit he was wearing earlier plus a shearling-lined denim jacket. I feel exceptionally stupid in my little dress, my teeth starting to chatter now. Like a girl who doesn't know how to take care of herself.

I have my speech all ready to go, and I launch into it before I can lose my nerve. "Listen, I was gonna say, I feel like I owe you—" I start, but Leon waves me off.

"Don't apologize just because I'm doing you a solid."

"I'm not just saying this because—"

"How about this: Don't apologize at all, okay? We were both moody today. It was dumb." He looks like he wants to say something more, and his eyes clock the goose bumps on my arms. But he just sighs, and I feel like I should let him get this over with.

"Okay. Well, it's, uh, the door in the back is the one I was hoping you could—"

"Lead the way."

I walk him through the little yard, and he climbs the steps there to see what he's up against. I stand at the bottom stair, trying not to hover while he works. The stupid feeling I got earlier blooms and grows in my chest, its heat the only warm part of my body. I'm desperate to do something to break the tension between us, to make this feel even 5 percent normal. "Can I at least apologize for interrupting your Friday night?"

That gets a little laugh out of Leon. He's been squatting in front of the door, staring down the lock; now he pushes his hair out of his eyes and glances up at me. I don't think I'm imagining that he gives my bare legs a quick scan.

"To be honest, I needed an escape," he says. "So technically, we're both helping each other out."

SQUARE WAVES

"Oh." I lean against the railing, shivering at the bite of the metal. "What were you escaping from?"

"My sister was doing a set at an open mic night earlier." I was expecting Leon to arrive with a full tool kit or something, but he pulls a couple of bobby pins out of his pocket. One he opens into a wide angle; the other he turns into a hook. "She was pretty good, actually. But our parents came, and she made some jokes about being second-gen and not feeling super connected to Korean culture, and that hurt my mom's feelings. And then they got into a huge fight, so I had to take Ruby out for drinks after to calm her down. You know. Family stuff."

He eases the hook pin into the lock and starts feeling around. *For what?* I wonder. When did he learn to do this? Why?

"That was good of you. To take her out."

"My sister is a drama queen." Leon rolls his eyes, but I can tell it's loving. "I've been refereeing her fights with my mom since I could talk. Typical middle sibling stuff, always trying to be the peacemaker."

I think of Leon as a kid, attempting to solve problems he was never going to be able to solve. Paralyzing himself with how hard he was trying to fix things.

He finds what he's looking for in the lock, and I hear a faint but audible *click*.

"Did you get it?"

"That was just the first one," he says. "It's gonna be a few minutes. You were at Willa's yeah?"

"Yeah."

"How was it?"

I shrug, but his back is to me, so he can't see. "It was a good party."

"Did you have fun?"

"That's an annoyingly perceptive question."

"You know me, Cass." Another faint *click*. "You can always count on me to be annoying."

I sigh. "No, you're not. I meant that you—" He's working faster now, and a third *click* comes right on the heels of the second. "I'm annoyed because you caught me being evasive."

He pauses to turn around and raise an eyebrow. "I know." Then he goes back to the lock, and I make myself let him focus. He keeps probing at it, patient, and for some reason, I can't breathe. It's like my body is remembering what it's like to be the thing beneath his capable hands, and there's nothing I can do to stop its response. He releases a fourth *click*, and then a fifth, before levering the lock into a turn.

The door pops open. I'm in.

Leon withdraws the pins and puts them back in his pocket.

"Do you just carry those with you everywhere you go?"

He laughs, and his dimple shows. "No, you got lucky. Since my hair's been getting long, I've been using them to keep it out of my face when I'm working at the wheel or whatever."

That's painfully cute. "Oh. Well. I'm glad you had them. And I know you don't want an apology, but I do owe you, like, a drink or something." I say it out of habit—because it's the thing you offer people who've done you a favor. But

Leon looks uncomfortable, and I wonder if he thinks I'm asking for an encore of our night out together. Trying to fuck my way out of our newly awkward dynamic.

"Sure. Sometime." Leon shoves his hands in his pockets. He's about to leave. He's already rejected my attempt to talk once, but I know that if I don't take this chance to try again—this weird midnight encounter, with no one around to witness us—I'll regret it.

So instead of stepping aside to let him pass me, I say, "Can I ask you a question?"

He nods.

"Did you really . . . did it really bother you, the way I was to you back in high school?"

A brief look of surprise passes over his face. At first, I think he's going to make a joke. Blow me off. But then he nods again.

"I didn't know."

"I didn't want you to know." He sighs. "And you weren't wrong about me, exactly, which is partially why it pissed me off. I was kind of a little shit. A slacker, and a stoner, and—whatever—that's the show I put on. I did waste a lot of people's time. Including my own."

I tap my fingertips against the railing. Being an adult is so much more complicated than I ever could have imagined when I was young and certain about everything in my life.

"Willa says you were a perfectionist."

"I got in my own way, that's for fucking sure."

"But then you stopped. Doing that."

"Did I?"

I expect him to be smirking, but he looks serious. Like maybe he's just as lost as I am. And as desperate for someone to tell him he's doing okay. So I say, "It seems like you did. I mean, you're so . . . good at things. And reliable. You do more for the store before lunch than I do all day. And when I needed help, I called you."

Leon refuses to smile. But I watch his eyes warm at the compliment. "I like being handy," he says, and I can hear the pride in his voice. "Being able to make things better."

"Yeah. It's"—it pains me a little to admit this, but I do—"It's cool."

A breeze brushes by us, and I shiver.

"You should get inside," Leon says.

"I should."

This time, he's the one who pauses. "Any chance you want that drink . . . now?"

We open my parents' liquor cabinet, and I contemplate the rows of bottles in front of us, but none of them seem at all appealing. "I feel like I'm in high school," Leon says. "Raiding your parents' booze."

"Listen, I feel like I'm in high school all the time now."

"You know what I really want?"

I blush, and I'm grateful he isn't looking at me.

He takes off his jacket. "Remember when you made us grilled cheeses after that party at Ellery's junior year?"

Drunk grilled cheese sandwiches were my high school

specialty; they're still one of the only things I'm good at cooking. "I do."

"You wanna make me one of those instead?" Leon puts on a puppy-dog face, and I laugh. I could use a snack myself.

Which is how I end up slicing cheese and hunks of butter in my parents' kitchen at one in the morning. Leon gets us glasses of water and hops up to sit on the counter, watching me at the stove.

"This is nice," he says.

"It is."

"We can be nice to each other."

My heart seizes with a memory of just *how* nice. My gaze darts up at him, to see if he's thinking what I'm thinking, but Leon is busy inspecting the package of oatmeal that's sitting on the counter. Probably for the best.

Neither of us says anything else until both of our sandwiches are on plates, sliced diagonally, and we're sitting across from each other at the kitchen table. Leon takes a bite of his. Then he puts it back down on his plate and props his forehead on the heels of his hands as he chews. "Fuck, Cassidy, this is as good as I remember," he mumbles. "And I was probably high when I had it the first time."

That startles a laugh out of me. "Oh, you were definitely high. I remember worrying that the couch was going to smell like weed in the morning." That was probably the only other time Leon was ever here: after a bunch of us bailed on a party when a rumor went around about the cops being on their way. My parents were out of town, we were in the neighborhood, and people came over to mine while we tried to figure out what to do next.

"Did I get you in trouble?" Leon asks now. His dark eyes are full of mischief.

"No." *Not like that, anyway.*

It's as if he can hear what I'm thinking. Leon smirks before he takes another bite of his sandwich.

"You know, I went to Bryce's birthday party a few months ago," he says after a minute.

"Oh?"

"Yeah. It was fun. But it was also—it felt like everyone there was so adult."

"I mean, we're all—"

"We're all twenty-eight," he says. "But there are a lot of different kinds of twenty-eight. Some of us are living with partners, buying houses, starting businesses. Some of us don't even know which of those things, if any, we want."

He glances at me, but his gaze flickers away too fast for me to really read it. Still, it occurs to me that Leon is offering me something. And that I want to offer him something in return.

There's no reason for me to trust him with this, exactly. But I do. "Did I ever tell you why I'm back?"

"I don't think you did."

I still can't believe the first person I'm admitting this to is Leon fucking Park. "Well. It's because I'm so burned out, I can barely do the most basic tasks. A couple of months ago, it was time for my annual review, and I was trying to fill out this questionnaire. It was going okay—strengths, weaknesses, etcetera. And then it was like, *What are you most looking forward to in the coming year?*" I take a deep breath. Even the memory makes my throat thick with tears. "And I just . . . didn't have an answer. Not at work. Not outside of work. My boss must have, uh, sensed that, because she put me on leave for three weeks. But I think . . . I think I can't go back there. And I have no fucking idea what I'm supposed to do next. Which is to say: I don't feel any more adult than you do."

Leon ate while I talked; now he puts his sandwich down. "I've been thinking. Maybe we should call a truce."

"A truce?"

"I know there's a lot that's happened between us. But while we're in the store, or with Willa, or even just, like, if something like this happens again—we can just. You know. Be normal. Not just ignore each other. Actually be nice. Actively."

I consider this as I wipe my greasy fingers on a napkin. I already promised Willa that this wasn't going to be an issue before I started. But this sounds like something verging on friendship, however temporary. Possibly even a chance to start fresh.

Maybe Leon and I don't have to keep poking every bruise we've ever left on each other's egos. We can accept that it *has* been a long time. That we've both grown—or tried to—even if we don't feel grown-up, exactly. And we can try to make the next week and a half not just bearable but actually pleasant.

"Yeah. Let's do it."

"Shake on it?" Leon offers me his palm. For a second, I want to say no. Touching him feels like crossing a bridge—like once I start, I might not be able to stop.

But that's silly. It's just a handshake.

I reach across the table, and his skin is warm against mine. I feel calluses I only half noticed, that night in his apartment. It doesn't have the same wild electricity of that contact; instead, there's a steady hum of pleasure, zinging under my skin.

WEEK TWO

X

I question whether one late-night conversation is actually going to change the tenor of things between us in real life. But when I arrive at the store on Monday morning, Leon gives me a nod and says, "Hi, Cassidy."

So, without prompting, I offer to help him paint the pedestals on Tuesday. We don't talk while we do it; he turns on the radio, and we both hum along as we work in companionable silence. Willa has been out picking up furniture from an estate sale—a curio cabinet that's her best find so far—and when she gets back and sees us, she just stands there for a minute, watching. "This is—I'm almost scared to jinx it," she says finally.

"If you get tired of ceramics, you have a future in mediation." I wink at her. "Maybe you could get, I don't know, Giants fans and Dodgers fans to paint a dugout in peace and harmony."

"I thought you weren't a Giants fan," Leon teases.

"I'm not."

"So you're the Dodgers fan in this analogy, then."

"Oh god no. I would never root for a *SoCal* team."

"At least you have some loyalty in that cold little heart of yours."

I can tell Willa is bracing for impact at Leon's taunt.

But I just shrug it off. "As long as we can agree that the Yankees are garbage, I'm fine."

Leon nods solemnly. "No one," he says, "likes the Yankees."

"Well, except Yankees fans," Willa observes.

"Garbage," Leon and I reply in unison.

Willa throws up her hands and goes to the back without saying another word to us, though I catch her muttering something about *parallel universes* as she walks by.

I try to take the good vibes home with me when I leave for my call with Tilly. It's been a week, and I was very much hoping to have something to tell her besides that I'm still not following her advice. That, in fact, instead of relaxing, I have taken up physical labor.

The clock ticks over to 4 p.m., and Tilly's office blinks into focus behind her on Zoom: its familiar, soothing, pale-pink walls. Her degrees lined up in a neat row, assuring me that at least one of us knows what the hell she's doing.

She starts off with a tough one: "How did relaxing go?"

"Um."

"Right. What did you do instead, exactly?"

"I sort of went and got a part-time job?"

Tilly throws up her hands, and I can't help laughing. "It's not paid."

"Does that make it better or worse?"

I rack my brain. "Better? Because I'm not doing it for capitalist profit motive?" I twist my hair off my neck. "It's a good deed. I'm helping out a friend."

"Sure. But where and how are you making time for *you* while you do that?"

"I have the evenings alone." I can feel myself putting on my *Cassidy has it all sorted* voice, and I try to tamp it down. "And . . . I don't know. It's been mind-clearing, honestly. To get out of my head for a little bit."

Tilly makes a face that I know by now means, *You are being avoidant, Cassidy*. But all she says is, "Does it make you think you might want to work in retail at some point? Or art?"

"Oh god no. But I did make a new list. Of, like, qualities I would want in a job. Stuff I value. Things like that."

"What's on it?"

I give her the rundown: Meaningful work. Flexible schedule, maybe not a traditional office job. I like interacting with people, but I don't want to do it in public anymore.

"Did writing that bring to mind anything you did when you were younger that used to satisfy those desires?"

I shake my head. In high school, I was mostly just . . . good at being in high school. National Merit Scholar, student government, that kind of thing. I prided myself in how many plates I could keep spinning: landing good grades, having fun, and getting into college. And once I ended up in DC, I let the city, practically a one-industry town, dictate what I did next.

My silence drags on for too long. "No," I say, finally. "I don't know. I've never had a dream job." I sigh. "I think the problem is that I don't like anything right now."

"Well, that's burnout for you." Tilly considers our options. "I'm wondering if maybe we should try looking in another direction. Do you have any mentors there in Berkeley, from growing up?"

Another *I don't know* isn't going to cut it, so I reply with the first name that comes to mind. "I guess an English teacher, Ms. Palazzo." I sort of worshipped her. Ms. Palazzo was older—in her sixties when I knew her—but the kind of older that made aging seem like it might actually be cool and interesting.

"It might be helpful to just . . . go all the way back," Tilly says. "Reconnect with yourself from then. As long as we're talking about values—where did yours come from? How did you develop them?"

The idea of revisiting the past makes me shudder. I don't *want* to reconnect with Before Cassidy. What could she possibly have to teach me? The goal is to move forward, ideally into uncharted territory. But I've refused or ignored basically every other piece of advice Tilly has given me, so I know I owe her one. "I'll try," I say, with considerably more optimism than I feel.

XI

I'm hoping that Ms. Palazzo won't remember me—or that if she does, she'll be the kind of person too disgusted by my notoriety to write back to an email. But the universe isn't on my side. Turns out, she retired last year, is "delighted to hear from" me, and is available for lunch on Thursday if that happens to work for me.

We meet up at a café a few blocks from the store. She looks exactly like I remember her: bright-eyed, with sharp cheekbones and exacting wardrobe details. Today, a crisp button-up with a set of slim gold bangles on her wrists. Her nails are done too, a cherry red, and she notices me noticing.

"I have time for a lot more personal upkeep now," she says with a laugh. "My daughter and I get manicures together on Friday afternoons."

"Oh, that sounds so nice," I say with a grin. But I feel a flash of guilt. My mom and I were close once, but we've lost that. My excuse is that I live on the other side of the country, but really our distance is because I basically refuse to come home to visit and have declined to share anything sensitive or real about my life with her since Cooper. I just don't want her to worry. What that means functionally is that we hardly talk at all.

Ms. Palazzo wags her fingers. "Well, my daughter insisted on it, really. At first I thought she was being silly. What do I need nice nails for, at this point in my life? But then I realized it wasn't about the manicure. It was about giving me some structure. Three weeks into retirement, I was clinging to that appointment like a lifeline."

"It is hard to imagine you not working, Ms. Palazzo." Back when I knew her, she never seemed tired or overwhelmed by all of the teenage nonsense that surrounded her. She had the unique trick of absorbing all of that nervy, hormonal energy and feeding it back to us as something that resembled calm.

"Jenny," she corrects sternly. "It was hard to imagine *myself* not working."

As we wait for our food orders, Jenny tells me about how she ended up in a high school English department in the first place, which involved dropping out of an English PhD program and doing a stint on Wall Street in the '80s—which she doesn't quite say but I think might have involved, like, a *lot* of cocaine—before landing where she did. I am honestly shocked, and it takes a little work to keep my face from showing it. Did I imagine her the way elementary schoolers think about their teachers—that they reside in their classrooms and have no lives outside of or beyond their work?

"It took me a while to realize that I *did* want to be in the academy, but not the ivory tower version of it," Jenny is telling me as our sandwiches arrive. "I liked learning, but I didn't want to spend my life in the archives, you know?"

I nod, still slotting all of the new pieces I have of her into place.

"But you haven't even told me anything about you. What are you up to these days?"

I toy with my napkin while I try to figure out how to respond. I'm past the point of my usual bullshit, I think; being semihonest with Willa—and then actually honest with Leon—helped me see that nothing will break if I admit that I'm struggling. But I also haven't figured out a new narrative. And I'm not sure I know how to function without a narrative.

"I've been working for an antibullying nonprofit for about six years now," I say. "But I'm actually thinking about leaving."

"Are you thinking of leaving for something, or just . . . thinking that you need to leave?"

"That I need to leave."

Jenny takes a sip of her water. She's been open and friendly this whole time, but now her face shifts, and I see her slipping back into teacher mode. "Are you looking for advice?"

"Not even advice, just—I don't know." Suddenly I'm sixteen again, words spilling out of me. "I'm kind of flailing. I'm looking for anything right now. Do you remember thinking I would be good at something in high school?"

Jenny laughs, but it's kind.

"This was my therapist's idea," I tell her by way of an excuse.

She nods. "Well, I think one of the things I learned early was that you never know where any given kid is going to end up. I mean, you have predictions, and sometimes you're right. But people change so much. I've been surprised too many times to give my inklings any credence."

"I can see that." I'm thinking of burn-it-all-down Zeke, now a dad with a buzzed head and a nine-to-five. Willa, an adolescent soccer star who hasn't played in years. Leon—well. Leon, who refused to invest much energy in anything at eighteen and now has more skills than I can remember, let alone name.

"I'm sorry I don't have better advice for you," she says with an apologetic smile. "The only thing I really know about adulthood is that everyone has to figure out how to do it for themselves. And almost no one gets it right on the first try."

It's not much, but it is a little reassuring. "I appreciate that. I know there's no magic wand or whatever. And I think even just saying this out loud to you helps." It isn't until the words are hanging in the air that I feel their accuracy. "Anyway, tell me more about retirement. Any new hobbies?"

Jenny's face lights up. And that's when I learn my seventy-two-year-old former English teacher is training to become a competitive weight lifter.

At the end of the meal, she excuses herself to go to the restroom, and I check my email to find a note from Jo, the guy I met at Willa's party.

SQUARE WAVES

Izzy gave me your contact info. Just wanted to say that it was so cool to meet you the other night. And I'd love to connect about opportunities with some of the kids I work with, either officially or un-. There's one in particular who had a cyberbullying incident last year, and I think talking to you could be really meaningful for her. But that's a big ask, and if you don't have the bandwidth, I completely understand!

I'm staring off into space when Jenny comes back.

"News?" she asks, gesturing to the phone still in my hand.

"Oh, no, but . . ." The question comes spilling out of me. "Can I ask . . . isn't it exhausting—dealing with other people's personal lives? Students and their problems, and then it's like, a decade later and someone like me is contacting you out of the blue, thinking you'll know what I should do with my life? Don't you ever get—just *tired* of it?"

I expect her to say something gracious and saintly about the rewards of service. Instead, she gives me a conspiratorial grin. "All the time. Especially when I was a new teacher. I basically just collapsed into bed at the end of the day. But the longer I did it, the more I learned that people are actually pretty good at working out their own problems. I didn't have to worry as much as I was. But also . . ." She takes a sip of water. "I think I got better at compartmentalizing. I created rituals. Simple things—just washing my hands when I was leaving for the day. Only wearing certain articles of clothing to work and never in my personal life. It's never cut and dried, of course. Some stuff will always follow you home. But I had to find a way to make space between the people who needed me at work and the people who needed me the rest of the time."

Then she levels me with a look I recognize: a *You'd better remember this; it's going to be on the test* gaze. "If you're asking if this particular meeting is a burden—no, Cassidy. I wouldn't have said yes if I didn't want to see you. And if there's one thing I am sure about—was then, am now—it's that you're tenacious. You're going to figure out what to do next. It might take longer than you want, but you will."

Against my will, a warm glow sweeps through me. How did I get so lucky, to have the support of women like Jenny, and Tilly, and Maya McPherson, who see the best in me, even when I can't see it in myself?

"I've had a weird life so far," I say.

"Honey," she says, cackling, "they're all weird, all the way through."

XII

As I walk back to work, the air is warm in the sun, cool in the shade—a perfect Berkeley summer day—and I mull our lunch conversation. Where my tenacity has gotten me so far.

Maybe part of the problem is that I throw myself so hard at things. I have no work-life divide in my current job. I answer emails from bed and on my phone when I'm on vacation. Donor events and speaking engagements mostly take place in the evening; they mostly involve dinner and drinks. And my role, ultimately, is to *be Cassidy Weaver*. What would it be like if I carried my personal hardships around in my personal life, and when I went to work, I got to put them down? Or at least tuck them out of sight?

When I think of Ms. Palazzo and a whole *classroom* full of kids—oof. I don't want to be a teacher. Too overwhelming. But when I consider Jo's teen . . . I kind of like the idea of meeting with her in an office instead of a coffee shop or randomly at a party. Closing the door so we could speak in private. Opening it again and letting both of us out.

When I step into the store, I pause to take it all in. I'm halfway through my time here, and it looks completely different than it did when I first came through the front door. It's fully painted and half furnished, with those Villeneuve pieces hanging in the far corner and making the room sparkle with color. New merchandise arrives daily; as soon as the shelving is all installed, it will be time to figure out where it goes. After that, we'll hang Leon's pictures—I'll get to see them. And then we'll be open for business.

Well, Willa will be. I'll get on a plane, head back to DC, and figure out what to make of my life.

I'm so swept up in surveying the space that I don't notice Leon coming through the door from the back office. "Hey," he calls. His hair is pulled away from his face with a few bobby pins, and it should look stupid, but instead it looks hot and feels . . . intimate.

"Hey."

"Admiring your handiwork?"

"Please. It's mostly your handiwork."

"Careful, Cass." He's smiling at me, big and wide, from his mouth to his eyes. Helplessly, I remember how he tasted, what it felt like to have those lips on my skin. "That was dangerously close to a compliment."

Our first conversation at the bar echoes in my bones. "Do you want a real one?"

He walks across the room casually, his hands shoved in his back pockets. My heart thuds with every step. "Are you kidding? Of course I do."

"This place looks great. That's in large part because of you."

He's a couple of feet away. Not quite close enough to touch. My fingertips are tingling anyway.

"And you, Cassidy, keep surprising me."

"I like keeping you on your toes." There's no mistaking the flirtation in my tone, and I blush immediately at my own words.

"You do, huh?" His voice is steady but—something. Leading.

My stomach clenches, and, god, I feel something sweet and scorching happening in my chest.

There's a noise from the back room, probably Willa hefting a box of clay, and it's a good reminder that we're not alone. And that we are technically coworkers—or at the very least, two people who promised their mutual friend that they wouldn't create drama.

"Where did you have lunch?" Leon asks smoothly, and I wonder if he was as aware of that moment as I was. If he's glad that it got broken or itchy and annoyed at having to get himself under control. Questioning what would have happened next if we had been alone.

"At Lulu's. With Jenny Palazzo, actually. English?"

He laughs out a breath, like *Of course you were having lunch with a teacher*. "Jesus. She hated me."

"I don't think she *hated* you."

"I always thought the two of you felt the same way about me actually. Slacker, loser, on and on."

"Did it ever occur to you that might have been a compliment in its own weird way? It wasn't just that you weren't trying. It was that you could do more. You weren't"—I break out the air quotes—"living up to your potential." Saying that makes me feel like I'm one hundred years old, but it's true.

"Why did you see her? A Leon Park 'living up to his potential' check-in?"

"We've been holding them weekly for ten years," I quip back. "Had to do it on Zoom while I was away, but it was great to finally be able to regroup in person." Then I sigh. "No. It was actually an *Is Cassidy Weaver living up to her potential?* meeting."

"And?"

"Jury's still out."

Leon shakes his head, like he doesn't quite know what to do with me. "Well, want to help me package orders while they deliberate?"

"If I get to be in charge of the bubble wrap."

We head to the back together. Willa is at the wheel, and she barely looks up when we come in. Either she's gotten used to us getting along, or she's too in the zone to care. Possibly both.

The big table in the center of the room is covered in finished ceramics: beautifully painted mugs, bowls, and plates. More complex serving platters. They've all been sorted by order with their address labels. Leon demonstrates the best way to make sure every edge is protected for their journeys on trucks, their inevitable tosses onto porches. I only stare at his hands a little bit while he works.

We have to share shipping supplies, but it's easy somehow. In the last week and a half, I've gotten used to being aware of Leon. Moving around his body in space. At first it was because I was avoiding him, but now it's something else. It's almost like a dance: him grabbing a piece of tape and passing the dispenser back to me or nudging a Sharpie in my direction just as I realize I need it. Willa has music playing, and I glance over and realize that Leon is mouthing along with the lyrics.

"Do you still . . . make music? Is that how people word that question?" I ask as I seal a box.

Leon laughs. "I mostly watch others 'make music' these days. A buddy of mine played Outside Lands last year, so we had backstage passes."

"That's cool."

"Yeah. We were in a band together back in high school." He shears off a length of bubble wrap with one easy run of the scissors. "Made our debut at the tenth-grade battle of the bands."

"I think I missed that." Once, I would have thrown my Jasper makeout in his face, just to see if he'd react.

"You didn't miss much. We weren't very good. Or I wasn't. Obviously he's talented."

I suspect Leon was too. Bailing on that one show hardly spared me from the sight of him sitting around on the benches at school strumming a guitar: the muscles in his forearms flexing, eyebrows crinkling with concentration. It really did feel like he lived to torment me then.

"Why don't you play anymore?"

"Eh, I liked learning an instrument more than the rest of it," Leon says. "Music was never really a passion."

"*Passion*," I repeat. "People are so obsessed with having passions. What if we just had jobs?"

"Well, Leon *is* an artist," Willa pipes up.

I think we had both forgotten that she was in the room.

"I'm not an artist," Leon says firmly. "I just like to make stuff."

"And I'm, what, anointed by the gods or something?" Willa lobs back.

"Anointed by Goop. Are you saying Gwyneth is a mere mortal?"

Willa rolls her eyes theatrically, and I get the sense that they've had this argument before. "There's no test to take. They don't give you a license. You don't have to call yourself anything if you don't want to. But are you really gonna tell me you spend that much time painting, and you don't care about it? You're making art, Leon. That makes you an artist."

"I mean, I do care about it, but . . ."

I can't tell what the expression on Leon's face means. He looks half pissed off, but half . . . pleased. Like he wants Willa to talk him into this.

She obliges. "It doesn't have to be more complicated than that. It really doesn't."

"I guess," Leon grumbles, but I can see it for real now: how much he likes the idea of being an artist. And how scared he is to admit it.

"Also, Willa, I was thinking for these cups—" He walks

over to her. "Do we want to try stacking them differently? Especially the ones with the crackle glaze?"

From there, Leon and Willa both get distracted by logistics, but I keep thinking about his paintings. I've seen so many unexpected sides of Leon in the last ten days. But they're decidedly practical: ways he's found to make himself useful. Now I'm curious what he does for the joy of it. What he makes because he can't help himself.

XIII

I'm grabbing my stuff to go home that evening when Willa comes bursting into the front room, fist-pumping. "Cassidy!" she shouts. "Cass! It's official! Richard Kerrigan just placed an order! And it's huge!"

"Oh my god!!! Congratulations!"

She sweeps me up in a hug, and we bounce across the room. I can almost feel the tension draining out of her body.

"C'mon," she says. "We're getting out of here. Bryce is putting together a picnic. We're going to meet at Indian Rock to celebrate."

"Damn, that's a throwback." In high school, Willa's parents lived a few blocks away from Indian Rock Park, and we spent a lot of time there: sitting in the grass, watching cute older guys learning basic climbing skills on the boulders, and furtively smoking cheap, shitty weed.

"I want to watch the sunset."

"You certainly deserve it." Leon. He's holding a jean jacket over his forearm, and his messenger bag is slung across his chest, highlighting the lean muscle there. Of course he's coming with us. And . . . I guess I might want him to.

SQUARE WAVES

Ever since he helped me with the lock after Willa's birthday party, something has been shifting between us. It's more subtle than seismic, but still, I can feel it: the ground slowly rearranging itself under my feet. Now my chest feels too light, like I've sucked in helium and accidentally turned into a balloon.

The three of us pile into my car and head into the hills. I haven't been to this neighborhood since I've been home, and every turn through the winding residential streets is a memory. In fact, this is the first place I drove myself after I got my license: straight to Willa's to pick her up.

In the past, when I imagined being back in Berkeley, I thought this kind of nostalgia would be suffocating. But weirdly, it's kind of comforting. It makes time feel expansive, wide open, and layered, instead of narrowly focused on the present and the immediate future.

Despite the summer-evening crowd at the park, we manage to set up where we have a view of the water, San Francisco and the Bay Bridge bright in front of us. Bryce shows up a few minutes later with a spread from the Cheese Board. We pour wine into paper cups, a little secretively, and I really do feel like a teenager again. Except that this time, Leon is on our blanket instead of sitting with some other group, his back to me in a way that couldn't have been—but always felt—deliberate.

"To Willa"—Leon raises his cup—"who's about to be an even bigger success. And who actually deserves it."

"To Willa!" Bryce and I echo. She blushes but doesn't object.

Bryce and Leon have apparently become just as good of friends as Willa and Leon have; they immediately start chattering about a sculpture show that Bryce read about. I lean against Willa's shoulder. "This is only the start for you," I say.

"Yeah." She doesn't sound half as excited as she did back at the store.

"'Yeah' what?"

"It just . . . doesn't feel like I thought it would."

"The opening will help, I bet. I mean, this is a truly crazy time to be trying to feel anything. You're too in it. Working too much."

She nods. "Sure. But it's also—"

Bryce leans over to interrupt. "Leon and I are gonna go climb for a minute," he says. "Want to join us?"

Willa and I shake our heads simultaneously. You can't grow up in the East Bay without doing at least a little climbing, but neither of us has ever taken to it.

The boys head off. I turn back to Willa. "But also what?"

"Oh, it's nothing."

"Doubtful."

Willa closes her eyes. "I'm just. So. Tired. And everyone keeps congratulating me and telling me how amazing this is. And it is! But it's also scary and overwhelming." She smears a palm across her face. "Everyone expects me to be excited and happy, and right now I just . . . can't. I'm sorry if that sounds ungrateful. But it's the truth."

I nudge her shoulder with my chin. "It doesn't sound ungrateful. It sounds honest."

Willa opens her eyes. She smiles at me. "It's really good to spend real time with you, Cassidy." Then she rearranges herself, recrossing her long legs, and I can tell she's not done. "As long as I'm being honest, I have to tell you, at some point last year, I started wondering if we were really friends anymore."

My heart sinks, and my jaw clenches. But her read—it's not wrong. What does it mean to be friends with someone who you never actually see, whose voice you rarely make the effort to hear?

"I mean, I will always love you, obviously. But our relationship had been mostly sporadic text messages for so long that I was starting to feel like maybe you were just going to fade away from me."

She holds my gaze. A signal that she knows this conversation is hard, but we're going to have it anyway.

"And then you said you were coming home . . . during the busiest three weeks of my life. I was like, okay, maybe it's a sign to let this go. But when you volunteered to help—when you showed up every day and busted your ass for me—it reminded me of why I love you. And why I wanted your friendship then, and why I want it now. So. Thank you for being this kind of friend to me again."

I press a hand to my heart; Willa does the same. "It's been different than I imagined, being back here," I admit. "Better. Like . . . a lot better."

Willa and I grin stupidly at each other for a minute.

Then she takes another sip of wine. "You go back to DC right after the opening?"

"A week from tomorrow."

"You must be looking forward to being there again."

"Yeah," I say automatically. And I do miss certain things. My apartment, with all of my books and clothes, and my shower with the good water pressure. Walking through the park on my way home from work—it's crazy, but part of me misses the wet, dense heat of DC in late summer. The way it makes me *feel* every inch of my body.

But I'm also realizing how rarely I see any of my friends there. I've done more socializing on this trip than in the last six months at home. In an effort to preserve energy, I had just kind of . . . closed in on myself. And it feels good to be opening up again.

I'm distracted from my thoughts by a shout: Leon, yelping with glee as he makes the leap from one boulder to another. His shirt rides up as he finds his footing. I realize I'm holding my breath.

Willa is giving me a look that I can *feel*. "You guys really are getting along lately," she says with studied nonchalance. "You and Leon."

"I'm as surprised as anyone, but. Yeah."

Her tone softens slightly. "It's nice."

"I'm sorry it took so long."

Willa laughs at that. "Listen, babe, me too. But also, I guess I kind of always thought—you know. You guys hated each other, but you were also clearly obsessed with each other."

Something happens on my face, and I try to hide it, but I'm not fast enough.

"Hah!" Willa cries.

"*Hah* what?"

"Please. You're blushing!"

Her accusation only makes it worse. I can feel how hot my cheeks are. "I'm not."

"Cassidy Weaver. Are you really going to keep lying to me about this? How many times do I have to say 'since we're being honest' or whatever until you spill?"

I really thought I was doing a good job keeping my feelings to myself. I bury my face in my hands. My heart zings in my chest. "Okay, listen. We ran into each other the night I got here."

"I knew it! I *knew* something was going on. Did you make out? What happened?"

"We slept together." My words come out muffled by my palms.

"*Cassidy*!!!" Willa is being way too loud. I emerge from my cocoon of shame to clap a hand over her mouth. She gives me big, sad eyes, so I remove it . . . slowly. She has the grace to look around guiltily before continuing in a quieter voice, "Was it good?"

"Unfortunately . . . it was so good."

Talking about it conjures that night in vivid, aching detail. Leon pressing me up against the wall outside of the bar, kissing me, lighting my bones on fire. His fingers moving inside of me, how he coaxed me to the brink of an orgasm once and then again. How satisfied I felt when he was fucking me, like I was finally exactly where I needed to be.

"And then? Have you done it since? Is that why you're suddenly—"

I shake my head rapidly. "No, no, no, no. I mean, it was supposed to be a one-night stand, and then . . ."

"Guess I really screwed that up for you. God, no wonder it's been so weird in there. Sometimes I thought about plugging you two into the electrical sockets. The tension could power a small *city*, Cass."

"I was trying so hard not to make it weird!"

"Well, you failed." Willa reaches over for the bottle and pours each of us another drink. She's been sitting crosslegged; now she pulls her knees into her chest. It's a habit I recognize from high school, and there's a pang of familiarity in my chest. "Now you really, *really* have to be honest. You're totally in love with him, aren't you."

"Oh my god, no!"

Willa looks skeptical, but I shake my head defiantly. I'm not in *love* with Leon Park. But . . . as we warm up to each other, it's gotten harder and harder to remember why we shouldn't sleep together again. And again.

And again.

"Well, listen. Obviously I don't know anything about anything. But as you know, I've always liked Leon. And he hasn't said anything. But I think he likes you."

I roll my eyes.

Willa gives me a look, like, *You are not playing it as cool as you think.*

I look over at the boulders. Leon is standing on top of one, reaching his arms up to the sky. His body is like a knife: sharp, useful. He stretches one leg out toward another rock, testing the distance. Seeing if he can make the leap.

The last time I chose someone romantically, I got it so utterly, catastrophically wrong. I know it's stupid that I'm struggling to open up even to Willa, but this is territory—emotional and conversational—I've worked hard to avoid. I blink hard. I put the disaster zone of my love life out of my mind and conjure all my self-possession. "Well. I think I might like him a little bit too."

Willa rolls her eyes. "Cassidy," she says, "I have been waiting to hear you admit that for fucking *years*."

XIV

We spend an hour at Indian Rock, and then another one. Eventually the wine is gone, and the sun is setting. Willa and I are lying on our backs, watching the sky's blue fade, when Leon and Bryce come back to our blanket. "We're hungry," Bryce announces. "Wanna get tacos or something?"

"Oh, absolutely." Willa sits up, shakes the grass out of her hair. "Tacos, Cass?"

"Tacos." I agree.

The four of us start gathering up plates and cups. We're all moving slowly, soaking up the last of the summer evening. I can't remember the last time I felt this unhurried.

Willa decides she's better off not driving—we're both pleasantly tipsy—and we all pile into Bryce's car. The backseat is big enough that Leon and I aren't touching, but I can still feel the warmth of his body radiating in the space between us.

"You guys have a good climb?" I ask.

He nods, gives me a goofy grin that flashes his dimple. "Nice."

"Oh, hey, you've got—" He leans over and plucks a blade

of grass from my hair. I have to resist the urge to turn into the contact. I glance at the rearview mirror, and I catch Willa smirking at me.

Leon twirls the blade of grass between two fingers. "Did you guys have a nice time lying around?" he asks.

"We had a really good conversation, actually," Willa says, all innocence. I swing my legs hard enough to accidentally-on-purpose kick the back of her seat.

"We did," I concede.

"About what?" Bryce asks.

"What success actually feels like," I say before Willa can try to slip in any little double entendre.

Pulling up to a dive bar with a taco truck parked out front halts the conversation. As soon as we get out of the car, I'm hit with the smell of onions sizzling in the fat from carnitas, and my stomach rumbles. Leon insists on paying for the food we overorder, and so I insist on buying everyone a round of beers. I go inside to grab them while the rest of the group takes our dinner to picnic tables set up out back.

I sidle up to the bar, flicking my hair over my shoulder. It's a bit of a cheap trick.

The bartender doesn't notice, but a guy a few stools down does. He's my age, maybe a few years older, with dark curly hair and big, broad shoulders. He looks like he could bench-press me one-handed if he felt like it.

"Hey," he calls.

"Hey." I turn another few degrees toward the bartender, trying to gently convey my disinterest. It's not this guy's fault I'm sort of exclusively into lanky surfer types recently.

"Can I buy you a drink?" he asks, a little more loudly now.

"Oh, no thanks."

"Why not?"

Jesus, he will not take a hint. I pivot to face him. "Because I'm here with some friends," I say. "And I'm actually buying them—" It's then that I realize my mistake. Because now this guy has had a chance to get a good look at my face. And to recognize me.

"Holy shit," he says. "You're"—he snaps his fingers—"Cassidy Weaver."

I've been experiencing variations on this moment for six years now. How I handle it depends on who, where, their tone of voice, and the look in their eye. My usual line for this kind of encounter—casual, glancing—is to smile brightly and say, "No, but I get that all the time. I must just look like her, I guess." But I'm so startled that it takes me too long to get the words out, and I can tell instantly that it's not my most convincing performance.

He narrows his eyes, clearly trying to decide if he's going to argue with me or not. But then I feel a hand on my shoulder. Leon. I step toward him, taking shelter in his body like a ship in a storm.

"Oh, I see," the guy says. He winks at us. "Nice work, man."

I flinch. Leon looks down at me, eyes flashing a mixture of indignation and concern. I shake my head. I'm not interested in any sort of redress aside from this dude leaving us alone.

Leon's mouth thins to an angry line. But he takes my

lead and leans against the bar so that he's blocking everything else from my line of sight. "I was gonna ask if you needed help carrying," he says. "But clearly you need help ordering. Once again."

I smile weakly. Roll my eyes for show.

"You okay?" he adds, his voice quieter.

I take a long breath, blow it out slowly. "I'm okay."

"Was he—"

"Just recognized me. That's all."

Leon shakes his head. Then he does something I don't expect: He reaches toward me, offering the curve of his arm for me to tuck into.

For once, I don't hesitate. I take the comfort he's offering and nestle myself against his body. I've never allowed myself the simple solace of anything like this: resting my head against his chest, closing my eyes to shut out the rest of the world.

I stay there while he motions to the bartender, orders everyone's beers. I inhale the smell of him, soak up his warmth, and take the time I need to compose myself. To recover from the shock of being reminded that even when I think I'm safe, if I'm in public, I'm always exposed.

I extricate myself to pay the tab. Leon tries to shoo me away, but I don't let him. "I've got it," I say.

To his credit, he believes me.

One of the many reasons I don't date is because of moments like these and how most men handle them. They puff up, get macho, disregard my desire to escape the situation as quickly and calmly as possible. They think they're responsible for me and somehow manage to ignore me—what I actually want and need—in their efforts to be my protector.

I watch Leon's back as we carry the drinks out to Willa and Bryce. The easy motion of his shoulders, his spine, his hips as he walks. The ease he has with his body and that he felt no need to use it as anything but an offering to me.

He shoots me one last questioning look as we sit down, and when I don't say anything, neither does he. Willa and Bryce are in the middle of a debate about flour versus corn tortillas, and we slip into that instead.

Once we've finished eating, Willa gets one last drink, Bryce heads to the bathroom, and it's just the two of us again. Leon was so bafflingly cool about the whole thing that I feel compelled to acknowledge what went down. "Thanks," I say, nodding vaguely back toward the bar. "For, you know."

"Yeah. No problem." Leon props an elbow on the table and rests his chin in his hand, regarding me.

"I hate it when that happens."

"No shit."

I laugh. "No, I know, obviously. But especially when it happens in front of other people. It always reminds me—" I cut myself off. There are too many ends to that sentence. It reminds me of what I did; it reminds me of how people see me. It reminds me that even people like Leon, who know the real me, have to know about all of that too.

"I'm sorry it's still so . . . heavy for you."

I have to drop my gaze to the scarred wood of our

table. Heavy is exactly what it is. And the way Leon held me earlier—how easily he took care of me then, how he's letting me talk about it on my own terms now—it's the closest I've come to feeling like anyone might ever want to, let alone be able to, help me carry it. The thought should feel comforting. Instead, it's terrifying.

XV

Richard Kerrigan's order is big, and he wants it fast—like, the next day. Which is fine except that his studio is all the way out in Stinson Beach, easily two hours from the store.

Willa offers to make the trip. Leon and I both roll our eyes at her. She has five days until her grand opening, and a lot of what's left involves decisions only she can make.

Which leaves the two of us. Leon will be fastest at loading and unloading all of the ceramics and second-best at talking to Richard, but Leon doesn't have a car.

"Well, but, Cass, you can drive, right?" Willa asks through a yawn.

I *can* drive. And I'm curious to meet this Richard and see his supposedly very cool house. But between my conversation with Willa and my interactions with Leon yesterday . . . the idea of having all of that time alone with him makes me nervous. It feels like we're on the precipice of something. I'm just not sure that I'm ready to see how close we are to the edge.

But Willa doesn't wait for my answer. "You guys go, I'm gonna see what I can get done here today," she announces with a nod that says it's settled. The only appropriate thing for me to do is get my keys.

Thirty minutes later, Leon and I are cruising across the bridge and into San Francisco. I put music on; I'm hoping that it will give us something neutral to talk about, like it did yesterday. But so far, no dice. I guess Dog from Hell is a touch too underground to be a conversation starter.

It's just after 10 a.m., but the morning's marine layer remains thick in the air. The city looks gray and cozy, all of its sloped hillsides crammed tightly with houses. It's not Manhattan, but still, it's dizzying to think about how many people live on this relatively small spit of land. How hard people fight to be this close to the coast.

"Have you ever been to Stinson?" Leon asks as I merge onto the 101.

"I don't think so." I've been to other parts of Marin County, but Stinson—which is mostly famous for its beach—was never really my parents' scene. "We drove down to Yosemite a lot when I was a kid. What about you?"

"My uncle lives there. It's where I learned to surf."

"That's so classic."

"Classic?"

"Just—so California. Learning to surf at Stinson Beach."

"I guess." Leon shrugs. "You talk like you didn't grow up here too."

"Sometimes I feel like I didn't. I've never even been on a board."

"Do you want to learn?"

"I'm pretty sure I'd be terrible. I've been doing Pilates for like a decade, and I still don't have much core strength."

"You need arms too. To be able to paddle."

"I don't have those either."

"Well," Leon says, "if you ever want to try, I'd teach you."

It's too easy to imagine: his hands on my shoulders, at my waist. Giving me a tiny adjustment here and there. His mouth next to my ear again, his breath hot on my skin. A tiny shiver runs down my spine, and I redirect the AC so it isn't pointing directly at my face.

We're heading into Tamalpais Valley now, following the 1 as it snakes toward the coast. I remember how much I loved this landscape when I was a kid: The trees, tall and dark and towering, felt like a protective netting, a canopy that covered me wherever I went. The sun is getting ready to poke through, lining the clouds in silver light.

We don't talk much for the rest of the drive, but the silence between us feels less charged. More comfortable.

This field trip feels like it was designed by the universe to get me to think more about my feelings toward Leon. And it's not *not* working. *But there's no future*, I remind myself. Just because I like being back in Berkeley doesn't mean my life is here. And if it were, what, would Leon and I just . . . date? Simply because we've finally put aside years of bickering and started occasionally being nice to each other?

You could at least fuck him again before you leave, the most annoying part of my brain reminds me.

When we get to the coastal portion of the drive, Leon rolls his window down, and the car fills with the scent of the sea mixed with eucalyptus. I take in deep lungfuls. I don't know what it means, exactly, but it is undeniable and not a little inconvenient how deeply this place feels like home.

Richard Kerrigan is a tall man, rangy and thin, with a craggy face and a Scottish accent that's gone soft at the edges after decades in America. He's wearing a chambray shirt tucked into a pair of faded Levi's when he comes out to greet us on his front porch.

"I'm so glad that Willa was able to get these to me so quickly," he says as we unload a box of serving platters. "I'm having a few people over for dinner tomorrow, and I really wanted to be able to show off her pieces."

"Willa's thrilled that you wanted them," Leon says. He seems genuinely awed by Richard in a way that's charming to witness. "Should we drop them in the kitchen, or . . . ?"

"Take them straight through to the back," Richard directs. "My assistant, Louisa, will catalog them for my collection. I keep track of everything I buy—even if I'm going to put a roasted chicken on it."

"I hear you have some of Roberto Lugo's early pieces," Leon says.

"Yes—though those have never made an appearance

on my dining table. I can show them to you when you're done unloading."

"You don't have to—"

Richard flicks his wrist. "That might be the only thing I enjoy very much, at this point. I've grown very curmudgeonly in my old age, I don't know if you've heard."

But he follows us through to the back room and chats easily with Leon while we unpack Willa's pieces. I'm trying to act like I'm not as impressed as I am with the house, but it's hard to hide my reverence. It's paneled in dark, glossy wood, but there are windows everywhere, endless panes of glass that allow the outside in. We're surrounded by trees, and beyond that, I can see the roll of the ocean.

When we're done, Richard takes us on a tour of his collection—or what's out, anyway. I don't recognize many of the names, but I can see why Willa was so excited that this man likes her work. He has incredible taste.

As awed as I am, I have an unsettled feeling, one that's familiar. I have the sense that Richard is . . . looking at me. In an *I recognize you but can't place you* way.

I doubt his scrutiny would be obvious to anyone else, but for me, it's impossible not to notice the way his gaze keeps sliding back in my direction, distracted. Like I'm a puzzle he can't quite solve. *You're being paranoid*, I tell myself. And maybe it's true. Maybe that bro at the bar is making me see things. But I'm pretty sure it's not just me. And the whole thing is another unwelcome reminder that wherever I go, there I am: Cassidy Weaver, a face you almost know.

A piece of scandalous pop cultural trivia. A person who makes you think of one thing and one thing only.

When it's time to say our goodbyes, Leon is practically beaming, in ecstasy over the whole experience.

"It was wonderful to meet you," Richard says. "I told Willa, but I'll say it to you too—I'm always looking for young artists to add to my collection, so if you come across anyone whose work should be on my radar, please do be in touch. I'm tired of buying up the big names, people who already have blue-chip-gallery representation and pieces in the collections of major museums. I want to spend the end of my career helping launch other people's."

At least one of us can have a dreamy afternoon, I think. "Leon is an artist," I say, the words falling out of my mouth. "A painter."

"Oh really!" Richard's excitement is palpable. "Do you have anything on you? A portfolio I could look at? I'd love to see—"

"I'm not that kind of artist," Leon says firmly. "It's just a hobby."

I remember that conversation he had with Willa yesterday. How it seemed like he wanted her to encourage him. Push him a little bit. I pipe up, "Yeah, but—"

"No," Leon says more sternly.

"Are you . . ." I trail off when I see the look on his face. Leon does not look secretive and pleased. He looks like he wants me to shut the fuck up. "Okay."

Richard shakes his head. "You've got a good one," he

says to Leon. "You're lucky to have a girl who believes in you like that."

If I was feeling the tiniest bit more surefooted, the look on Leon's face would make me laugh. He's trying to figure out how to put Richard off without making him feel worse, and all he can do is stutter. "Oh, I'm not—she's not—"

"We're friends," I say, and I realize, to my shock, that it's actually . . . true. Friends who had sex once, but still: genuine friends. We've never been anything remotely close to this before. It's kind of a big deal.

Leon seems to think so too. "Friends," he repeats, like he's testing the word to see if it will hold our weight.

"Friends is good," Richard says. "Friends is good too."

With our awkward finale officially wrapped, Leon and I head back to the car. We climb inside; I put my key in the ignition but don't turn it. "Sorry about that. I didn't mean to—I guess it probably came off as—I was just trying to be nice," I say, turning my body toward his.

Leon sighs. "I know that." He stares straight ahead. "But trust me: I'm not Richard Kerrigan material."

"Okay."

There's a pause. Leon runs his hands through his hair. "It was nice," he says. "Ill-advised. But nice."

I start to turn the car on but then stop again. "To be honest, I'm jealous that you have any direction at all. A thing you like doing. I'm still totally at sea."

After my conversation with Ms. Palazzo, I had the thought that maybe I might like being a therapist. Or a psychology researcher or something. But as soon as I started looking up the graduate school involved, I got overwhelmed and intimidated. There are MFTs and MSWs, all kinds of master's programs; to become a psychologist, I'd have to get a PhD. I closed all of the tabs and haven't opened them since.

For a second I think Leon's going to touch me—my shoulder, my arm. But he doesn't. Instead, he leans back in his seat, tilting up his chin. "I know the feeling."

"Does it go away at some point?"

"I'll let you know if I find out."

I glance over, and Leon is just looking at me—this simple, open expression I don't think I've ever seen on his face before. Like there's no hiding here. He's not trying to be anything other than what he is. There's just us and this moment. My heartbeat starts to pick up.

Friends, I repeat to myself. We've just successfully achieved that milestone. No need to try to blow past it to anything else. So I start the engine and back out of the driveway. A text from Willa pops up on the car's touch screen.

Leon's phone buzzes in unison, and he reads the message. "It says . . . *Are you guys on your way back?*"

Another buzz.

"Oh, shit. She says there was a big accident on the 1. Traffic is extremely fucked."

"Well that sucks."

"She says—" He pauses. "She says we should probably just hang out here until it clears."

"Oh." I try to make my response as neutral as possible. Every minute I spend with Leon feels like an endurance test. How long can I go without stepping in it again? Making it weird? Without kissing him square on the mouth?

Leon seems unbothered. "I'm pretty hungry actually. There's a spot near the beach bar that I used to love—maybe we can eat and try to wait it out?"

The café is quaint and classic, with a white-painted wood exterior and surfboards hung on the ceiling.

The waiter brings our waters, and I bite my lip. "Can I ask about your art a little bit? Just like, in a normal way?"

Leon relaxes back in his seat. "Of course."

"When did you start drawing?"

"I mean, I always did, I guess. Just doodles and things. I took a few classes a couple years ago, got more serious then. I mean, I don't know how serious I am, really. But that's when I started, you know. Trying."

Leon has been wearing his sunglasses; now he lifts them up so I can see his eyes. "Can I tell you the truth?"

First Willa, now this. It's like the universe is trying to send me a message about honesty or something. "Of course."

"When you brought up the senior art show the other day—I think about that a lot." He fiddles with the salt and pepper shakers. "And you probably know this at this point, but I feel like I should say, I really wasn't trying to pull a prank or anything. I wanted to hang something. I wanted—" He laughs a rueful laugh and doesn't finish his sentence.

I pick up where he left off. "Well, it drove me crazy, watching people laugh at your joke. Because it landed. And from ten years' distance, I can admit that it was funny. But at the time, it made me feel so stupid. Like there I was, trying my ass off. And all you had to do was fuck up, and everyone loved it."

"Not everyone." Leon's gaze catches mine. His eyes are dark, fierce. The air between us shifts, going tight with tension.

I act on impulse. "What were you going to say, before?"

"What do you mean?"

"You said, 'I wanted.' And then you stopped."

Leon closes his eyes. He looks like he usually does when his gaze finds me: slightly pained. But also like . . . maybe he's kind of enjoying it. "If I tell you, I'm going to need you to promise not to hold it over my head forever."

"I can't make that promise."

"Wow. Okay. Then I can't tell you."

"No!"

Leon shrugs. "I gave you the conditions. You refused them."

"I'm just being realistic, okay? I could have lied to you. But I didn't. Don't I deserve some credit for that?"

Leon shakes his head, like he's tired of my nonsense. But then he takes a deep breath. "Part of why I got in my head so badly then is that I wanted you to know that you were wrong about me. I wanted—God!" He looks away, then back at me. "I really wanted to impress you."

"Impress? Me???" I can feel myself glowing. Gloating.

Basking in the smug sense of victory I feel. Rubbing it in and not pretending otherwise.

"This was a mistake."

"You're right, it was. You will never be able to untell me that."

Leon is blushing, and it takes everything I have not to reach out to touch his cheek, to see if it feels as warm as it looks. "Somewhere, back in time, high school Cassidy is smiling, and she doesn't know why." I shimmy my shoulders, preening. "But she will. Oh, eventually, she will."

"I mean, don't get me wrong, I still hated you. But that's why I signed up for the show in the first place. I thought if I could show you what I really thought about—that I was more than just, you know, lazy—you'd be forced to admit that you were wrong about me. But I couldn't do it, obviously. And that ate at me for years. *And* the fact that I'd gotten away with it. That that was all anyone expected of me. For a while, I thought it was all *I* could expect of me."

I know a thing or two about disappointing yourself. About letting a personal failure color your whole life.

"So is showing at Willa's . . . your redemption narrative?"

"I'm trying not to put that kind of pressure on it," Leon says. "But maybe there's something there."

"Well. I'm looking forward to seeing it."

"I'm looking forward to you seeing it."

I'm fairly certain that the next thing that comes out of my mouth is going to be way too sincere. But the waiter shows up with our food, and our fish tacos break the spell.

XVI

"Traffic's clearing up, but it's still kind of gnarly," Leon reports from Google Maps after we pay.

"We could take a walk? The beach isn't far, right?"

"About five minutes from here."

"Let's go see the water. And then we can head back."

We're off without another word, and when we get to the sand, it's fairly quiet—a handful of families with kids playing and surfers starting or ending a session. There's a lineup of them out past the break, their wetsuits making them look sleek and dark like seals.

Leon stares longingly in their direction. "Man, I wish I'd brought a board. Or even just my trunks."

"Isn't the water freezing?"

Leon raises an eyebrow at me. Then he starts toeing off his sneakers. He reaches down to pull off his socks before I truly grasp what he's about to do.

"You are not."

"I can swim in my underwear. I don't think anyone here will be, like, offended."

I survey to see if anyone's looking at us. They aren't. But this still feels dicey. The day has warmed up, but it can't be above seventy-five.

"You're going to sit in the car the whole way back in wet boxers?" I ask, eyebrows arched.

"I'll take them off."

He sounds completely innocent, but still, my breath catches in my throat as I imagine one less layer of fabric between us. How easy to let my hand drift over to his thighs and then between them. "Come on, Cassidy. You're on this coast for, what, another week? And you're not gonna at least touch the Pacific?"

I jog a few steps over to where the tide is coming in, all foam. I dip my fingers in. I was right; it's frigid. I dash back to flick the seawater in Leon's face.

He just laughs and shakes his head. Like we're playing. Like I just made the first move in a game.

When I realize his hands are at his belt, my throat goes dry. Images from that night have taunted me for the last two weeks, but this is like one of them coming to life before my eyes. Every fantasy I've had since is suddenly way too close, too clear.

When I pull my shirt off over my head, I'm partially trying to distract myself. Well, distract myself and also make sure that I don't let Leon win at anything. Even if that thing is a polar plunge for no good reason. My boy shorts can probably pass for bikini bottoms, my bralette is mostly made of lace, but like Leon said, no one's paying enough attention to take offense.

"The trick is to just get in before you have time to think about it," he says, gaze locked on the waves. "Don't psych yourself out. Just . . . run. On three. You ready?"

"I'm not!"

He gives me a teasing grin and starts to count us down anyway. "One."

I cannot believe I'm doing this.

"Two."

I really, seriously cannot believe that I'm about to do this. In order to what? Prove a point? Divert my attention from the miles of tan skin next to me, the muscles in Leon's thighs tensing in anticipation, the musk–salt–Old Spice scent of him that I've been hung up on ever since—

"Three," Leon calls, and I run.

The water is sharp against my toes, my calves, my thighs. The tide rushes around me, and I almost stall, but Leon is pulling ahead of me, diving in, getting swallowed by a wave, so I push forward and follow. His timing is perfect: The current rushes over us, and when I emerge on the other side, I'm breathless with exhilaration.

"What the fuck!" I yell in his general direction.

Leon's hair is plastered back from his face. He looks younger. More like the boy I used to know. "Fuck yes!" he yells.

"This is insane!!"

"Feels good though, right?"

I have to admit that it kind of . . . does. The water is so buoyant that I barely have to tread to stay afloat. Sunlight glints off each ripple, silver dancing against the dark.

"Another wave is coming," Leon says. "Swim out a little bit. We want to get under it."

I follow his lead: duck when he tells me to duck, jump when he tells me to jump. Part of the reason I've never loved the beach is because I don't really know how to navigate the ocean. But he gets us out past the break, where it's calm, where we can just bob like corks. My fingers are going numb at the tips, and yet . . . I have to admit that I haven't been this joyful, this present, in a long time. It's Friday afternoon, and I'm not in an office. I'm not cocooned in my bed, working from home, doing camera-off Zooms; I'm not stressing about a budget or a presentation or my stupid future. I'm half naked and completely free.

Leon is laughing, and I realize I'm laughing too. At nothing. At everything. At how utterly absurd it is that we're here at all, let alone together.

Being out here with him almost feels like lying next to each other in the dark: cloaked by anonymity, wrapped in something that's as soothing as it is scary. And I realize: It's time for a confession of my own.

"I wanted you to think I was cool!" I yell out.

"What?"

"In high school. You wanted me to be impressed by you. I wanted you to think I was cool."

Leon dips under the waves for a moment, and I can't see how his face responds. When he emerges, he shakes his head. "What a pair of dorks."

"Ha. Like anything's changed since then."

"Oh, I can think of a couple of things."

SQUARE WAVES

Something brushes against my wrist in the water, and I brace for a jellyfish or a gross patch of seaweed. But then I realize that it's Leon's hand, reaching for me. He threads his fingers through mine. Squeezes.

Then he swims away, toward the shimmering horizon. I watch the muscles in his back move. He isn't gym-built like some of the guys I've been with; instead, he's graceful, like he knows every inch of himself. Like his body is meant to be put to use.

"I'm getting out," I call after him. "I can't feel my toes anymore."

"Wimp!" Leon responds, but he's only a few waves behind me, and we wash up on shore at almost the same time.

Our underwear seemed passable as bathing suits before we got wet. Now the cotton is clinging to Leon's hips and ass and outlining his dick in high definition. As cold as it was out there, it doesn't seem to have affected him much.

"That wasn't so bad, was it?" he asks.

"No, no it wasn't." I mean it, but I'm distracted.

Leon looks away from me. I wonder if he noticed—how could he not?—the way my nipples are pressing against the thin lace of my bra. A shiver ripples through me at the idea of his attention there. His hands there. His mouth there. I feel a tug in the lowest part of my stomach, and I realize I am wet everywhere.

"There's probably a blanket in the back of the car," I say. "My dad is big on disaster preparedness."

"Mmmm." Leon studies me as if trying to assess me for the next steps. Beads of water slide down my ribs, along my hips, between my legs, and he appears to be closely tracking their movement. The white noise of the waves crashing around us drowns out everything else and makes it hard to remember we're not alone. His tongue swipes against his bottom lip. I don't think I've ever felt this observed—or this needy.

Channeling my best Bond girl, I pull my hair off my neck and twist it into a rope, wringing it out.

That seems to bring Leon back to himself. "Yeah," he says. "Car. Let's do that."

We walk back, barefoot and dripping, with our clothes bundled in our hands. I'm torturously aware of the precise distance between Leon's body and mine. If I thought I was turned on that first night when he pressed his knee against mine, I don't know what I am now. I'm like a firework, waiting for the briefest touch of a match to set me off.

In the trunk of the car, we find a full emergency kit with water, energy bars, a radio, a flashlight, and a fleece blanket that doubles as a towel. Leon flings it around me like a cape, rubbing it up and down my shoulders.

"Damn, what a gentleman."

He rolls his eyes. "It was my idea for us to go into the water."

When I look up, I realize how close our faces are. "It was fun," I say.

"It was." Leon's hands have slowed. One drifts from my shoulder to the bare skin of my collarbone. He tugs on a lock of damp hair, and my inhale catches in my throat. "I can't believe I'm saying this. But it's been fun hanging out with you, Cass."

I can't help prodding a little bit. "How much fun?"

"Sometimes too fun. And I think maybe I'm forgetting—what we are to each other."

"What are we?"

He could step away. Break the moment. Make a joke. I could too. But I don't.

"High school rivals," he says. "Enemies."

"Former enemies. I thought we landed on friends."

"Right. Friends." Leon's been holding the blanket up; now he lets it drop. One hand comes to rest on the crest of my hip, and I feel the contact like a brand.

He helped us navigate in the water, and I can handle it here on land. "We're also—" I keep shifting closer, closer, until his thigh is sliding between mine. I lock eyes with him. "We also fucked, that one time."

"We did." I'm close enough now to feel Leon's ribs move when he inhales. "I haven't forgotten," he murmurs. "I haven't stopped thinking about it since. How good you felt. How hot you looked bent over in my bed. How much I want to do it again."

The hand that's pressed against my hip squeezes, a possessive little clench. I shudder. Bury my face in his neck. "God."

"And I think—" He rolls his hips into me, and my legs spread automatically, making space where I want him. "Sometimes I think you want the same. But I'm not sure.

And I don't want to push. So I just keep . . . waiting. Trying to be friends with you until you tell me I can be something else."

"It's been excruciating," I say. And then I kiss him.

As my mouth moves against his, I realize how much better each touch feels now that neither of us is fighting against anything. Neither of us is spending energy maintaining a front. I'm not half furious at myself like I was the first time; I'm not tipsy and exhausted and trying to hold back. I have no idea what happens next between us, but I know I can stop pretending that this isn't what I want.

He fumbles behind us, shoving the trunk closed so he can press me up against it. I would laugh if I wasn't so incredibly turned on. Then we're a blur of limbs: Leon's hands on my waist, greedy, like he can't get enough. My legs wrapping around his hips, urging him closer, closer. There's almost nothing between us, and I'm panting into his chest.

It's only the sound of a truck backing up a few blocks away—its steady *beep, beep, beep*—that forces me back to myself. Public sex has never been my thing, but I'm so aching and empty right now that it's hard to remember that we are in public. I pull away from Leon, trying to catch my breath. His eyes are hazy, his mouth swollen; I'm sure I'm the same.

"We should . . ." I sigh. "Not do this here."

"You're probably right." He stands straighter, but then he dips his head to nip each of my nipples through the salt-soaked fabric of my bra.

"You have no self-control."

He grins up at me, self-satisfied. "Never have."

For a moment, I consider just pressing his hand between my legs, the two of us getting me off together before we have to drive back. It would be so simple to slide my underwear to the side, to guide his fingers to my swollen skin, hot against the damp chill. I know how talented his hands are, how easy it would be for him to tip me over the edge.

But if there's one thing I do not need at this point in my life, it's a second sex scandal. So I disentangle myself from him. This time, Leon doesn't pretend he's not looking, and his stare lights me up everywhere.

He's shameless when he reaches down to readjust himself, not that there's really anywhere for him to go in his wet boxers. "You're going to kill me," he says.

Now it's my turn to be cocky. "Yeah, well, what else is new?"

XVII

After we climb into the car, Leon slips a hand into my lap, but the parking lot setting kills the vibe enough for me to bat him away. I don't want to come with half of my mind on what people can see through the window. Especially not when we have plenty of privacy in our future.

We spend an agonizing hour on the road. When we get back to the store, either Willa notices that my hair is tangled and salt crusted and she keeps it to herself . . . or she's too distracted that the bathroom sink is clogged to pay us any attention.

Knowing she's in her own world is like a hall pass for Leon and me to drop our act. We brush up against each other every chance we get; each time our eyes lock, one of us smirks. It's embarrassing and thrilling and stupid, and when we leave two hours later, I'm too wound up to do anything other than ask Leon to remind me of his address.

Walking through the front door, it's the first time I've seen his house in the light of day; it's nicer than I had imagined it would be before. There's the same jumble of shoes in the entryway, but the floors are swept clean. There are vintage furniture pieces in the living room, the kind of Craigslist finds people brag about scoring. When we pass through the kitchen, the sink is empty and gleaming.

"How many people live here?" I ask.

"Three. Well, four if you count Ryan's boyfriend, who's like, a semipermanent resident."

"Four."

Leon pushes the door to his room open. "Yeah, well, it's a lot of rent."

Do I have to always sound so fucking judgmental? "I didn't mean—"

"I don't really care what you meant," he says, and then he's kissing me again.

I'm desperate to get my hands on the skin I could only look at earlier, and we're both immediately pawing at each other's clothes. I shed my top, and I get his jeans pushed halfway down his thighs before he eases me back onto his bed, unbuttons my pants, tugs them off me, and slings them over his desk chair. He's already kissing his way down my body, drawing one of my legs over his shoulder, his intent perfectly clear.

"We should—" I say. "You should—" But then his mouth is on me, hot and slick and consuming, and the rest of my words are lost in a guttural groan.

Leon holds my hips tightly, pinning me to the bed while he covers every inch of space between my legs with his tongue, his grip on my thighs firm, authoritative. If I felt exposed before, shivering in my underwear on the beach, it's nothing compared to now, when he has me completely naked, spread out like a feast. His right hand releases its hold on my leg, and I feel his thumb press against my clit, moving in a circular motion. My thighs begin to twitch, and I shake in his grasp. There's a buzzing between my legs, a shimmering, pulsing sensation that moves up my torso, building with each steady flick of his tongue, each stroke of his fingers.

"Leon," I say, calling his name like I want him to do something other than exactly this. I can't turn away from him again, and I don't want to. Whatever this is, I'm giving myself over to it completely. He pushes two fingers inside of me, making a motion that creates friction against the most sensitive part of me, and I am catapulted. My head thrashes on the pillow; my hands flex, grasping at nothing. "Fuck, fuck, oh my—"

I come apart, pleasure rushing through my entire body so hard that all I can do is tremble my way through it.

I press my palm to my cheek, as if to steady myself. It takes both of us a minute to catch our breaths. Leon eases the rest of the way out of his jeans.

"You really—you really like doing that, huh?" I roll over to cover his body with mine.

"Especially to you." He reaches up to cup a palm to the underside of my breast. I reach down and take his dick in my hand, where I can feel his pulse is running ragged, just like mine.

"You said that the first time too. It seemed like maybe . . . you'd thought about it before."

I give him a purposefully coy look and start sliding my

hand up his shaft. Leon flings his free arm over his face. "At some point, I thought about it every day. You were always so in control, and I just—I've wanted to see you let go so badly."

I smile. "And? Now that you've seen it?"

He shakes his head. Pinches his lower lip between his middle finger and his thumb. "You're still driving me crazy, Cass. I mean, have you ever tasted yourself?"

My heartbeat picks up, and I realize I'm feeling something more than pure lust. Behind the want running wild in my veins, there's something deeper—almost tender. As if I need Leon to know me and *like* me. Really like me.

I push the thought away and kiss him. Deeply, hungrily. Until we're both panting again, his hips angling toward mine, his dick agonizingly hard and pressing against me where I'm so soft and wet. I slide myself back, then forth over his length.

I have no idea how he drags himself out of bed to get a condom; all I know is that I feel the loss of his body under mine like it's something essential to my existence. I roll onto my back and watch him, the assured lines of him and the places where he's vulnerable too. When he comes back and covers my body with his, his expression is calm but hyperfocused, fixed on me. He grips my hair in his fist, and I tilt my chin to align my gaze with his. He slides into me with our eyes locked, and he keeps me there, like there is nowhere else to be. He fucks with the same slow, steady rhythm as the first time, and it's just as maddening.

Then his thrusts turn stronger, rougher. The bedframe

knocks against the wall, and I press my palms behind me, both to brace my body and to try to soften the noise.

"Leon," I muster, "what if—"

"Probably not home," he responds. "And anyway, that's what headphones are for."

He pins my wrists over my head, and I gasp, shifting my body lower and trying to get him deeper. The first time we did this, I hid in the shadows and attempted to pretend I wasn't feeling as much as I was. This time, I'm throwing my whole self into it. My jaw goes slack, my eyes roll back against closed lids, and I clench around him, coming again, this time more slowly so that I feel every inch of it: the hollowing out of my lungs, the steady pulse of my walls squeezing around him.

Warmth spreads through me as he comes, the throbbing of him inside of me matching my pumping heart. I lap up every detail: the final stutter of his hips. The way his mouth falls open and his eyes squeeze shut. He's usually so graceful, but just in this moment, he's inelegant, wild, and it's stunning. Fuck.

He kisses my shoulder and then settles himself at my side.

The silence is comfortable. I examine myself for signs of regret or shame, but there's nothing. Just the sweet satisfaction of an afterglow: half well-fucked fullness and half anticipatory hunger to do it again.

Leon rests a hand on my thigh, both casual and proprietary. "Are you going to bolt again?" he asks.

"I wouldn't say that I *bolted*."

"Please. You were out of here before I got the condom off."

"I didn't want to wear out my welcome."

"You didn't want to admit how much you liked it."

I can't argue, so I bare my teeth at him; Leon bares his back. Then he nudges his nose against mine and kisses me, full and sweet.

"I think you knew how much I liked it," I say, catching my breath.

"I liked this time, not having to wonder, much better."

It's dark out by the time we stumble down to his kitchen. We're both starving; Leon says he'll make something. From a counter stool, I watch him chop garlic and ginger into perfectly uniform tiny cubes, rinse rice, and get the cooker going. I like observing him work here just as much as I do at Willa's. The easy competence of his body, the fluid way he moves through space, his lack of a recipe—it's all hot.

Now that I'm less distracted by imminent sex, I turn back to how I felt in Leon's bedroom. How I'm feeling now, to be honest. That there's more than just chemistry and sexual tension between us. It turns out that fucking someone I like enough to even try to be friends with is very different than a one-night stand with a guy I despise. And I have too little actual dating experience to have considered that until right now. Did we just graduate from one-night stand to easy fling or something . . . else? Something more?

The thought makes my chest tighten. A familiar sensation of panic starts to vibrate just behind my breastbone.

This is your fear of commitment, the well-therapized part of my brain says.

This is your right mind, telling you not to trust Leon Park!!! screams the rest. It starts cataloging his faults as he cooks for us, sautéing chicken and cabbage and toasting sesame seeds in another skillet. *Just because he's charming—and sensitive, and open, and good at taking care of people—does* not *mean—*

It's easy to tell myself that I'm being afraid for no reason. I've logged enough hours with Tilly to have mastered that. It's much harder to actually fight fear when it comes at me like this. The warning bells ringing through my body that something is *wrong, wrong, wrong.*

I soothe myself with a familiar mantra: I'm leaving so soon. There's no chance for this to really grow into . . . whatever. I can be with Leon while I'm here. I do have a future to worry about, but it has nothing to do with him.

He slides our meal across the kitchen island to me on ceramics that look very familiar. "Did Willa make these?"

"I did."

On second look, that's actually pretty evident. Willa paints her pieces with wobbly, colorful stripes that have a human touch; Leon finishes his with a bold, clean, almost machinelike grid.

He grabs a half-full bottle of wine from the fridge and two cups that match the plates. "They're porcelain. Nice to drink from." He winks. "It'll feel good in your mouth."

I'm about to say something indecent back when the front door bangs open and two of Leon's roommates walk into the kitchen together.

"Hungry?" Leon asks, settling into the stool next to mine.

"No, we went out," one of them says, a guy with a closely shaved head and an earring dangling from one lobe.

"It was getting a little loud up there," the other, taller with piercing eyes, adds, smirking at Leon and then me.

"Sorry." Leon tries to hide his smile and look cowed. "Also. This is Cassidy."

And here's where my hard-earned shamelessness comes in handy. I hop off my seat and reach out to shake each of their hands. "I tried to tell him," I say grinning. "But you know Leon. He's stubborn."

XVIII

Leon and I spend the night in his bed, and on Saturday morning, we decamp to my parents' house, where we can make as much noise as we want without bothering anyone.

In theory, anyway. In practice, it just feels . . . wrong. Looking down at the duvet cover in my teenage bedroom on my hands and knees or sliding between Leon's legs to get my mouth on him while we watch a movie turns out to be more mindfuck than turn-on, and we end up back at his place on Sunday afternoon.

I'm sprawled naked on his bed while he picks up clothes off the floor. Straightening and tidying. Making up for the fact that we've done very little aside from fucking over the last forty-eight hours.

By now, the clutter of art on the walls has started becoming distinct to me—I've dissected the backdrop of framed posters and paintings and how they've been slowly crowded out by sketches and doodles, some of them no larger than a Post-it note. "Who did that?" I ask, pointing to a painting on the opposite wall.

"I did."

I sit up and shift to the edge of the bed so I can see it more clearly. "Wow. It's gorgeous." It's of the sea, and he's layered blues and greens to capture the way light moves on water, the endless, textured topographies of it. There's something anticipatory to the scene, too, that I can't quite put my finger on. Looking at it reminds me of how it felt to stand next to him in the sand. How badly he wanted to dive into the waves and swim.

"Thanks."

"Are the rest of them all you too?"

"Not all of them. The photographs are by my friend Buckley. And a lot of the framed stuff I bought or did as trades with people."

"But the paintings—" I stand up and start to examine them. Just as quickly, Leon is behind me. He does what he did the first night: wraps his arms around me, kisses my neck. But I'm not willing to be distracted this time. I disentangle our limbs, gently but firmly. Leon pouts, rolls his eyes.

It hits me then how long we've known each other. Even though we used to argue more than talk, even though I was determined to think the worst of him 100 percent of the time. I've been reading his facial expressions—his body language—god, I've been *looking* at him for so long.

And that means I know when he's nervous.

So I hold my hands out to him, palms up. "Let me see them?"

Leon pauses. I watch his ribs as he inhales, exhales. He nods.

He goes back to putting away T-shirts while I make a slow circle of the room. In one corner, he's tacked up some stray pieces of graph paper: studies for future paintings, I assume. They're all familiar scenes: skate spots, shoreline. There are a couple of small paintings above his dresser: portraits of his roommates and one of Zeke—mohawk still intact—that sends a pang of sentimentality through me.

When I'm done, it's my turn to wrap my arms around Leon. His skin is warm against mine, and the weight of history—his, mine, ours—is easy to forget in moments like these. Whatever happens next, I'm glad we got here. "They're really special," I tell him.

He gives me a bashful smile. "You have to say that."

"You think just because you go down on me now, I won't be honest with you?" I pull back a little bit. "Are any of these going up at the store?"

Leon shakes his head.

"Well, I can't wait to see what is."

"Yeah. Me too." Now he looks nervous again. Not just nervous; evasive.

I glance around the room. There's no pile of fresh sketches on the desk or stack of canvases waiting to be framed. If what's on his walls isn't going to hang at Willa's . . . there's no sign of stuff that is.

Before I can ask, Leon's phone dings with a text. "Speak of the devil," he says. "Willa says she found a plumber who can come in first thing tomorrow morning to look at the bathrooms. Jesus, what a nightmare. Though I guess worst-case scenario we just shift the opening a few days."

Suddenly, I find I'm very interested in the stitching on the bed's top sheet. "Yeah. Well. Hopefully not too far. I would love to be there."

"Mmm." Leon's brows furrow. "Right."

We haven't talked about that at all, really. Leon knows I'm supposed to leave a few days after the store's big debut on Wednesday, but we haven't discussed what that means. I don't want to, and so far it hasn't seemed like he does either.

Leon taps out something to Willa and puts his phone down. Then he says to me, "Hey, you want to go out to dinner tonight?"

"Out? Is that . . . you asking me on a date?"

"Sure. And just—might be good to reintegrate ourselves into the world a little bit."

"I guess that would require wearing clothes," I say, pulling on my jeans. "Of which I have very few."

Leon hands me a sweat shirt from his stack, the one he was wearing at the bar when we ran into each other that first night. It's cloud-soft, and even though it's freshly washed, I can still smell faint traces of him. That spicy skin scent that I've grown greedy for and can't even allow myself to think about missing.

We walk over to a little Japanese place, an izakaya where Leon knows the owners, a husband-and-wife team. The wife, Mai, is the bartender; she's working on a fall cocktail menu and insists that we sample most of them with our meal. We split every glass, and by the time dinner ends, I'm full and tipsy. We linger even after we've paid the check, just sitting and talking and making eyes at each other.

"That was so good," I say, leaning back. "It's going to be hard when I have to go home and cook for myself again and eat DC produce. The Bay has been very good to me, food-wise."

"Oh, just food-wise?"

I knock my ankle against Leon's under the table. "Dick-wise too."

"Ha. My dick appreciates the compliment."

We're sitting next to each other in a booth, and I take the opportunity to grope him just a little bit, over his pants.

To my surprise, he grabs my hand, threading his fingers through mine, turning my crude gesture into something sweet. And that anxiety rises up again. That fear.

So I untwine our fingers. Kiss Leon on the cheek. Say, "We should probably head out. I should get back to my parents' place."

"Really?" He looks surprised.

"They get home at the crack of dawn tomorrow. I don't want to have to answer questions about where I've been sleeping." It's the truth, but it's also the half-truth. I'm an adult whose parents already know way more about her sex life than most. What I don't want to answer questions about—from them or from myself—is what's going on with me and Leon, exactly.

Leon nods, his head bobbing. "I'm going to go to the bathroom, then we can walk back."

It's a perfectly innocuous response. But the way he looks when he says it—it's a little closed down. Like he was almost hoping I'd give him something more.

WEEK THREE

XIX

When I wake up in the morning, my parents are already home. I can smell coffee brewing in the kitchen and hear my dad bustling around, conferring with my mom about various pieces of mail that arrived while they were away.

I give myself five minutes to stare at the ceiling, unmoving. Seeing my parents—especially at home—always feels like a head-on collision with the ghost of Before Cassidy. They loved her better than anyone. But what's really crazy is that they love After Cassidy too.

At first, when the scandal was still fresh, I almost wanted them to be mad at me. To be as furious with me as I was with myself. Now I just feel guilty about everything I've put them through—and how much I pushed them away in the process. I guess that's an improvement, but not by much.

I make myself get up and brush my teeth. I put on clothes and head downstairs where my parents are sitting at the kitchen table. They look way better than they should for a pair of jet-lagged sixty-somethings. Probably better than I do. My dad's "There she is!!" is so loud and joyful,

I wince. "We slept on the plane!" my mom announces as she hugs me. "Ambien is a wonder drug."

"Don't worry, we won't be so chipper this afternoon," my dad assures me. "Do you want breakfast? We were thinking about making eggs."

My mom again: "They cook them in *so much butter* in France."

I take a second to appreciate their easy back-and-forth. Whatever my romantic fuckups and hang-ups are, they sure aren't my parents' fault.

"I'll take some buttery eggs. Can I help?"

"I need to stretch my legs," my dad says. "You take a seat. Tell us how everything went while we were gone."

I give them an edited version: working at Willa's. Taking some time to think about my "career goals" and realizing that I might need to "reassess my priorities," which is the code I've settled on for easing them into *Surprise! I hate my job, and I need to leave it.*

I feel weird about not bringing Leon up at all. But they read me too well, and his is a name they'd recognize. I'm terrified that as soon as I say it, they'll ask the right questions, and I'll give myself away. I'll reveal, at least on my face, that there are feelings there—and that I don't know what to do with them.

Of course, they're not combing my stories for holes. They're mostly excited to tell me about their two weeks in Paris. They hit the Louvre, the Eiffel Tower, and Père Lachaise and ate just about every pastry they came across.

My dad is telling me a story about a museum full of

taxidermy when I realize I have to go if I don't want to be late. "Sorry," I say, grabbing my bag.

"I'll be here all week!" he jokes. "And so will you!"

I have no idea how I feel about that—add it to the list—and I give them both a kiss before I head out.

I want to check in with Leon—make sure the cloud that passed over his face last night has dissipated. But when I arrive at the store, there's no time. The drain issue seems solvable, but for the time being, we don't have an operational bathroom, and the plumbers have rearranged everything in the back room, so we also can't find anything we need.

The only good news is that they assure us that we should be in shape for our Wednesday opening. Two days from now. I throw myself into the work so hard that eventually it's 3 p.m. and I haven't eaten lunch.

I grab a sandwich Willa ordered earlier out of the fridge and go to the parking lot in back. It isn't remotely scenic, but I need a break from the bustle and noise inside the store.

I'm playing a dumb game on my phone when I see a call from a number I don't recognize. Normally I wouldn't pick up, but Willa has been trying to arrange a drop-off with a florist, and since she's out running another errand, she gave them my number instead.

"Hi," a voice on the other end of the line says when I answer. "Is this Cassidy Weaver?"

Did Willa give them my name? My full name? Alarm

bells start to go off, but I'm still too distracted—too deep into my current world and reality—to identify their origin.

"Yes."

"This is Mark Treinen calling with *Us Weekly*. We're running a story about Cooper Abbot getting remarried, and I was hoping to get your comment on—"

"Fuck *off*." I end the call, but my hands are already shaking.

I crouch down and press my back against the metal door. I drop my head between my knees. Sometimes, no matter what I do or how far I pull myself away, it all comes flooding back. The chased-animal feeling of being cornered and terrified. My brain repeating on a loop, *This is bad, this is bad, this is so bad.* How it felt to see my own flirty texts in black-and-white newsprint. Leggy, pouty-lipped pictures of me pulled off Instagram and shoved onto tabloids' bright pages. The mix of fear and guilt and heartbreak—because I was, briefly, stupid enough to believe that Cooper Abbott loved me. How I spent the whole first day waiting for him to call and say, *Don't worry, babe. We'll get through this together.*

I fucked up so badly once. I cannot fuck up like that again.

I block the number that called and tap through to find an old familiar setting on my phone: Silence Unknown Callers. I'd switched it off just six months ago, thinking I was finally in the clear. Oh, sweet, naive Cassidy. The public's attention span is short, but its memory is long.

I'm still out there when Willa's car pulls up. It's probably only been ten minutes, but it feels like hours.

"Hey," she says. "I ended up stopping by the florist to grab the—" She gives me a look that lets me know that whatever I'm feeling, it's showing on my face. "Are you okay?"

I nod like a puppet on a string. I'm not, but she has enough on her plate right now. I force a smile and hope it looks at least mildly convincing. "Totally," I say. "Just tired. Are the vases in the truck? I'll grab them?"

I spend that evening, and the next, at Leon's house. When we have sex, I focus on how it feels in my body and experience the pleasure there. And for brief stretches of time, I get to ignore everything happening in my brain.

But I don't stay the night. Every time I try to imagine telling my parents that I'm seeing someone—let alone Leon—an icy panic starts to wrap around my chest. I get the same sensation when I think about telling Leon about the phone call. Part of me really wants to. I'm sure he would be good about it, the way he was at the bar. Let me say whatever I needed to say. Feel what I needed to feel.

But really opening up to him about how complicated this part of my life still is would also mean broaching another layer of intimacy, one that feels like a burden. Sometimes I get so sick of having to manage my mental health and *deal* with my *trauma*. I have enough regular problems without diving into all of my special ones.

I'm aware that I'm not making the best decisions. I let myself make them anyway.

XX

When I pull up to the store on Wednesday morning, it's buzzing with activity. For weeks, the space has belonged almost entirely to me, Willa, and Leon. Now it's crawling with strangers: caterers bringing in trays of food and guys in black T-shirts setting up a bar. The sudden loss of our cozy summer camp vibes takes me by surprise—my rational brain knew this was coming, but not how it would make me feel. I fight the urge to mourn the closing of that minichapter and fight even harder to ignore the fact that it's the prelude to the end of my trip. Now's the time to focus on being my friend's hype girl.

Willa is standing at the center of the room training the women who will be working the register, students she found by posting flyers around campus, and there's a team bringing in heavy, framed paintings and leaning them against the walls. I walk over to her during a brief pause in the chaos and grab her arms. "Holy shit! It's all really happening!"

"Yeah," she says, her eyes wide. "It is." She looks like it's all really hitting her: sort of excited, mostly overwhelmed.

I nod at one of the men handling a painting. "I didn't realize you had art coming from anyone other than Leon."

I mean, I'm guessing here, but these are *very* different from what he had in his bedroom. The one that's currently being hung is abstract, large scale, a little dark. Next to that sits a carefully rendered portrait of a woman in a dentist's chair.

"Oh yeah, that happened really last minute. Actually—" But she's interrupted by someone with a question about where they should store the ice. Then someone else is at her side to report that the internet is on the fritz.

I touch Willa's shoulder. "Tell me what I can do to help."

She closes her eyes for a second, and I can almost see her sorting through her mental to-do list. "Will you see if you can find the box of shirts that arrived the other day? I want to make sure they don't need to be steamed before we hang them up."

"Of course." I give her shoulder a squeeze before letting go.

"Thank you, Cass."

I head into the back room, where the box was almost certainly shoved into a corner when it arrived during the plumbing emergency. I'm also hoping to find Leon, give him a hug, and maybe catch a glimpse of his paintings before they're up for all to see.

I spot him as soon as I walk into the room. He's in the corner, chatting up a vaguely familiar-seeming older man, both of their backs to me. Leon has traded his usual worn-in Dickies for black twill pants. His collared shirt fits his shoulders perfectly, but he's still himself: There's a Giants cap keeping his hair out of his way.

He lights up when he sees me, and all I can think is that as good as it used to feel to annoy him, it's so much better to make him beam. "Cassidy!" he waves me over.

His companion turns around, and I realize why he seemed familiar. It's Richard Kerrigan. He nods in greeting. It's a perfectly friendly gesture, but there's something slightly stilted about it. An awkwardness that makes me think that, in the space between our first meeting and our second, he figured out where he knew me from. The inkling feels like a needle, scratching at my skin. All of the unease I've been trying to ignore settles, cold and insistent, at the base of my skull.

I smile brightly. I will make this interaction comfortable if it kills me. "Richard! It's so good to see you again. I didn't know you were going to be here, but I'm sure Willa is thrilled." Last I heard, he had a dinner that conflicted with the actual party. Maybe he decided to pop by early to check out the space anyway.

"I didn't either," Richard says. "But Leon called last night, explaining that some work that was supposed to be hung up had gotten delayed, and I thought—how could I say no?"

Everything slows down as my brain connects a series of unpleasant dots. "Delayed," I repeat. But I would know if anything was held up. If we were waiting on anything other than Leon's paintings.

SQUARE WAVES

I look at him, willing him to give me some other explanation. "Richard loaned us some really exciting pieces," he says.

"I'm happy more people will be able to see them," Richard adds.

The bottom falls out of my stomach. I feel so stupid, standing there, my congratulations for Leon slowly fading from my tongue. When did this happen? Why didn't he tell me? Why didn't he try harder to make it *not* happen? What happened to his redemption arc?

What happened to being so different than he was all those years ago?

I don't have to deal with Leon right now, I tell myself. *Willa needs me.* "That's so cool. Do you guys mind if I slip behind you?" My voice is coming out strangled, too high, but I plow ahead anyway. "Willa asked me to grab something, and I think it's right—" I point to a maroon shirt poking out of a half-opened box.

Leon watches me, but if he has questions about my tone, he doesn't ask them.

Instead he asks, "Can I help?"

"No." I heave the box into my arms. "I don't need anything from you."

Before I know it, it's 6 p.m., and I'm in the bathroom, changing into the dress I wore to Willa's birthday party. When I chose it, I'd been hoping that Leon might remember, compliment me on it, maybe slip a hand under the skirt, just briefly: a promise for later.

But now I don't even want to look at him. I'm so annoyed—pissed, in fact—that he didn't take this opening seriously enough to deliver what he was supposed to. *Procrastination* was one thing when we were teenagers, but all anyone's told me since I got here is how much he's changed. The fact that he couldn't get it together for Willa—on today of all days—is pretty serious evidence to the contrary.

I finish tugging up the zipper at my back and give myself a once-over in the mirror. My hair is long and loose and golden over my shoulders; the dress is a simple navy that's polished but still fun. I look nice, I think. I still look like I have my shit together, even if I absolutely do not.

I open the bathroom door, and Leon is standing there. Judging by the look on his face, he agrees with my self-assessment. "Wow," he says.

He leans in to kiss me. And at the last second, I turn my head so that he just catches the edge of my mouth. I know I'm being bitchy. I start to give him an excuse about not wanting to mess up my lip gloss, but I stop myself. This is probably the last quiet moment before the party starts. I either say something now or keep stewing and make things awkward all night long.

"Can I ask you something?" I start.

"Yeah." Leon reaches up to hook his fingers over the edge of the doorframe. It only emphasizes how lanky he is, and I feel a flash of familiar desire to press my palms to his exposed strip of stomach. To nudge my forehead into his neck and pretend everything's fine, actually.

But I've done enough pretending.

"What happened? With your paintings?"

He shakes his head. "I've been working on them for months. But nothing felt right. And I thought I would have more time this last week to work through some new ideas, but when we—"

"Oh, so this is my fault somehow? That I've been a distraction?" The anger I've been trying to keep at a simmer leaps to a boil.

Leon's hand drops, and he takes a half step back from me. "Hey. That's not at all what I meant. I was just saying—something happened. Things changed. And listen, Cass, something came to me that I do want to paint, that does feel right, but it requires more time." He scans my face to see if I'm softening. I think he can tell I'm not. "And anyway—Willa and I talked about it. She gets it. I made this loan happen with Richard, and he called a guy from the *Chronicle*. So now they're going to report on the opening. How Willa is bridging the old-school Bay art scene and the new one."

My only response is a frustrated shrug.

"Why do you still seem upset about this?"

"Because I am upset! Because—" I start. But I can't bring myself to say the next words. *Because if you fail Willa, you will fail me too.*

Leon hears plenty in my silence. "You know, I thought

we had agreed to be over our high school bullshit," he says. "But it's like you're looking for something like this. For some reason to remind me that no one will ever forget that I was a fuckup first and foremost, you most of all. Do you need me to be embarrassed, Cassidy? Will that make you feel better?"

"That's not what I—"

Leon takes a deep breath. "Listen. The party's about to start." He's lowered his voice. "Let's not do this now. To Willa. We can talk about it tomorrow."

He doesn't wait for a response. He walks past me into the bathroom and closes the door in my face.

I have to go outside to collect myself. I snag a glass of wine from the caterers on the way. It's a chardonnay—never my preference—but that doesn't matter because I can barely taste it.

How *dare* Leon act like I'm being unreasonable for asking a simple fucking question. About something he told me he was committed to doing and then *didn't*. Instead he covered his ass like he did with *Procrastination*. And is patting himself on the back and getting credit for it in the same way too.

The more I ruminate, the angrier I get. Clearly we've both been fooling ourselves all week, thinking we could *grow* and *change*. There's just too much history here, and good sex does not erase that.

I'm leaving in a few days anyway. I'll leave Leon and

whatever feelings I had for him here. Shove him out of my head like I've done with so many things. Go back to my stupid messed-up life in DC and . . . attempt to fix that, I guess.

The thought is like a pinprick to the balloon of my anger, and suddenly all I can feel is how sad and tired and scared I am. Tears gather in the corners of my eyes.

My phone buzzes in my bag with a text from Izzy: *Jo and I are here. Where are you??*

I take a deep breath. I blot at my undereyes with my fingertips. Leon was right about one thing: I have to get through the rest of the night without Willa worrying about me even once. Tomorrow I'll sort all of this nonsense out.

So I affix a mask of cheerfulness to my face. Check my camera to make sure my mascara hasn't run and fluff my hair. Then I go inside, where the party is starting.

XXI

I've just finished giving Izzy and Jo a tour of the store when my parents arrive. Their first order of business: finding Willa and showering her with praise. Then they want to be shown around too. I point out the pedestals Leon and I painted, the wheel and the kiln, and my favorite pieces by Willa and the other artists. The absence of Leon's work on the walls is glaring.

My dad is just as entranced by the Villeneuve chandeliers as I was the first time I saw them. At this hour, the sun is at the wrong angle to illuminate them, so Leon hung a light that shines through them and covers this corner of the store in swaths of pastel.

I can't wait to get out of this place, where everything is a reminder of him.

"Don't we need one of these for fruit?" my mom asks, touching the edge of one of Willa's larger bowls with a gentle fingertip.

"I think we do," my dad agrees.

As he goes off to pay, my mom lingers behind with me.

"This is pretty amazing," she says.

"It really is."

"I'm so glad you were able to do so much to help."

"Oh, I mean, I didn't—"

"Willa says you did."

"I was only here for a couple of weeks."

"Still, Cassidy. I guess it's also that it's nice to see you involved in something that you seem to have . . . enjoyed."

The tears I thought I had curtailed earlier come rushing forward, but I blink them back. My mom has always been tender with me, even when I was putting my whole family through hell. I want so badly to prove that she was right to believe in my ability to come out the other side.

I let her wrap me up in a hug. As we pull apart, I hear someone clearing their throat into a microphone. Willa is standing on a step stool and trying to get everybody's attention.

It's a packed enough party that it takes a minute or two for a hush to settle over the crowd. A server is handing out glasses of champagne, and I snag two and hand one to my mom.

"Hi, everyone," Willa says. There's applause and a stray whoop. Leon, I guess. She blushes, fans herself. Someone's wolf whistle splits the air. "Okay, okay, enough of that. I really just wanted to say thank you. Because my name is on this store, and my ceramics are for sale. But this never could have happened without my community, and their work, and their love and sacrifice. My sister, Cerise, and her kids, Jackson and Tavi. My parents, Curtis and Leslie." She indicates a knot of smiling family members, who accept some applause of their own. Her dad takes a little bow. "My Bryce." Even from this far away, I can tell her eyes are wet.

"And I would have been dead in the water—especially these last two weeks—without my friends Cassidy and Leon."

My mom is beaming and directing a silent golf clap toward me, but all I can see is Leon across the room. His gaze locks with mine, and I feel everything. Every scorching kiss he's pressed to my skin. And all of the fear and disappointment and hunger that's been gnawing at me for weeks now. It's so much bigger than him. Than us.

"And of course," Willa continues, "I will never be able to offer enough thanks to the artists who have given me the honor of showing and selling their work here." Leon and I are still looking at each other. He nods, and we slip through the crowd, out the door, and into the night.

It wasn't quite three weeks ago that Leon and I stood outside of a different front door. I was two drinks deep then too, but mostly I was using tipsiness as an excuse to do what I'd maybe always wanted to. To let myself be just a little bit reckless with him.

Now I'm just . . . wrecked.

"Good party," Leon says.

"Good party," I agree.

We look at each other for another long moment. He takes off his hat. Ruffles his hair.

"I'm sorry," he says. "About earlier."

"Yeah, well. Same."

He takes a step toward me, but I stay planted. The smile that was starting to bloom on his face falters and then falls.

"I'm flying back to DC on Friday."

"I know."

"And I have no idea what I'm going to do from there."

Leon looks at the ground between us as if he's sizing up the distance.

"I can't be . . ." I continue. "I can't be thinking about you. Or Berkeley. Or high school. I need to go back to my real life."

He looks hurt. And a little insulted. "What about this isn't *real life*?"

"Well, I don't have a job, for starters. I've just had all of this time to hang out with you and, like, fuck around."

Leon's eyes narrow. "So that's all this was. Fucking around."

"Listen . . ." I sigh. "I'm glad this happened. I'm glad to have gotten a chance to actually get to know you and like you. But tonight—we just keep misunderstanding each other. I don't want to trap either of us in the past. And I think the easiest—the best—thing to do is to let each other go, so we can move forward."

Leon's jaw tenses. "I mean . . . if that's how you really feel, then fine. But that's not how I feel. And I think—honestly, I think you're just scared, Cassidy."

My anger flares. "And since when are you my therapist?"

He sighs. "I've known you for a long time. And I know

you don't want to talk about this, but I'm not eighteen-year-old Leon anymore, and I'm not Cooper Abbot either."

The sound of his name in someone else's mouth—the reminder of how public my pain is—finally snaps something in me. "Don't you dare say that name to me."

Leon looks chastened. But he doesn't back down. "I'm sorry I overstepped. But am I wrong?"

He's not, and we both know it.

"I just can't—I can't do this with you." My voice cracks. I feel like I'm going to crumble where I stand. "For a million reasons. Cooper being one of them. My life's a disaster, Leon. And I can't figure it and you out at the same time."

He takes a step toward me. But that's as far as he goes. "You don't have to . . ." he starts and then sighs. "You've made up your mind, haven't you?"

"Yeah."

"Okay. Well. I know better than to argue with Cassidy Weaver when she's dead set on something. But for the record, I thought what we had was real. And I wanted more than this."

My eyes trace the planes of his face. I look for his dimple, but it's nowhere in sight when his expression is so worn down and sad. "It was real," I say. "And also, can you just trust that I know what's best for me?" I try to shift my eyes off him, but I can't bring myself to do it.

Leon looks like he wants to argue. But I asked for something, directly, and he's going to give it to me. So he turns around. I watch the breadth of his shoulders, the line of his spine, as he walks away from me.

SQUARE WAVES

Then I press my forehead against the store's cool exterior brick, and I finally let the dam break. I'm crying about everything, now: how scared I am that I'm twenty-eight and washed up. That I'll never figure out what to do with myself. That I'm too hurt to love anyone else well. I'm crying because someone hurt me when I was twenty-two, and it's like they say: Grief is a spiral. I keep moving further and further away from it, but I still have to pass the same points on the circle every now and again, and I hate it every time.

Eventually, the tears slow and then stop. I'm left with the worst thing of all: the truth I didn't want to admit to Leon or myself. That it's not just men I don't trust when it comes to love.

It's also me.

XXII

I always forget that crying is like throwing up: Avoiding it is worse than getting it over with. When I wake up at 7 a.m., my eyes are still puffy, but my head is clearer than it has been since . . . I can't remember when, actually.

Light filters through the windows. I can hear birds chirping. It should be perfect. Peaceful. Calm. Instead, I'm itchy with the desire for escape. From here and from myself.

I want to put on a podcast. Play a game on my phone. Go to the store and see if Willa will put me to work again. This is exactly why I ignored Tilly's advice when she advised me to slow down and relax. Because I knew I couldn't bear being alone with my thoughts.

Now I have no choice.

I ease myself out of bed, as if it's my body that's sore instead of my heart. Then I go downstairs, looking for a chore, something to occupy my hands while I think. Unfortunately, my dad must have emptied the dishwasher before he left for work this morning. The counters are sparkling. There's even coffee in the pot for me, still warm.

I pour it into a mug and sip it while I try to plan what

I'm going to do next. I canceled my therapy session this week, claiming a packed schedule spending time with my parents. I'm trying to figure out whether I should ask for a makeup when I hear the front door open.

"Hey," I call out.

"Hi in there," my mom calls back. A few years ago, she cut her work hours in half, preretirement, and she's probably just getting back from her morning walk. She comes into the kitchen, her cheeks rosy from exertion. "You're up early! I thought you might sleep in, after the party last night."

I shake my head. "I didn't end up staying that late."

"Oh." She's dumped the dregs of her coffee from her thermos, soaped it, and rinsed it clean. Now she turns around to look at me. "I don't want to bug you, but—is something going on, Cassidy? You seem a little"—she looks me over, searching for the right word—"lost."

I almost laugh. *Lost* is exactly what I am. And after all of the time I've spent hiding, it's a relief for someone to find me, to see me so perfectly clearly. "Yeah."

My mom nods and opens the fridge. "Well, I was about to start marinating some chicken for dinner tonight. Want to help me prep it and tell me what's going on?"

It occurs to me that I come by my *keep busy* ethic honestly. "That sounds nice."

"Excellent. Chop four cloves of garlic, please."

"You got it." I grab a head from the hanging basket over the sink and a chef's knife from the block. Its weight feels good in my hand. Stabilizing. I shake the reminder of Leon's perfectly chopped garlic out of my head.

"So."

I'm too exhausted to do anything but tell the truth. "I know I said this sabbatical was a reward. But the truth is, I've been really unhappy at work. Like, really, really unhappy. And I think I might quit my job when I get home."

My mom has pulled like fifteen different ingredients from a cabinet: sesame oil, soy sauce, fish sauce. I can't even see what else. "Okay. Go on."

"And I have no idea what I'm going to do next. And also—I've been seeing someone while I was here. Or was. But he was—we were—" I pause. Take a deep breath. "It fell apart last night. And it's just like . . . am I going to be this broken forever?"

"Oh, baby." She abandons her marinade to come give me a hug. "Do you really feel broken?"

I grab a paper towel to wipe my eyes. "I don't know. Kind of. Yes."

"I don't think you're broken. I think you're brave."

God, that fucking word. "Well, I disagree."

"I know you do, sweetie. But consider: You are very close to your own life. And sometimes it's easier for other people to see things like that."

I shake my head at her. "Don't you ever get tired of having to support me?"

I'm half joking, but she's completely serious when she responds. "No. I wish you would let me support you more. For a while, I thought maybe you were talking to your friends about this sort of thing and that that was enough. Then I hoped your therapist was breaking through. But over the last few years, I've started to wonder if you've just decided this is yours and yours alone to face."

I don't know what to say to that, so I go back to the garlic.

"I'm serious, Cassidy. Very few people have seen, up close, what you went through. And how hard you've worked ever since. To be okay. To help other people. To—I don't know. Make up for it, I guess. I'm not surprised that you're tired and overwhelmed. It's a lot to take on every day."

It's exactly what I want someone to tell me, and that somehow makes it hard to hear. It makes me feel like I've tricked her.

But I know what Tilly would say about that. So I take a deep breath. In, out. "Thank you."

"Also, for the record, if you do decide to leave your job, you're always welcome here. The house is so quiet with just me and your dad."

In the wake of the scandal, I refused to move home. It felt too much like admitting defeat. I have that same instinct now: to refuse her offer. Insist on asserting my independence. But I've been doing that, and I can't say it's served me in the ways I'd imagined.

I'm not ready to say yes yet. But I let the idea of having it as a backup plan take root in my mind. It's nice to know that there's something—someone—who will catch me if I fall again.

"I'll think about it," I tell her.

When the chicken is back in the fridge, we decide to go out to lunch together, and she heads upstairs to shower.

I get ready, and then I make myself sit still for five whole minutes.

The inside of my head is *so. Loud.* I wonder how the store is doing. I think about whether I can get out of my lease in DC. I consider if I even want to do that. I ask myself if I could ever come back here.

And then the timer on my phone goes off. I have not meditated. I have not achieved nirvana or inner peace. But I have been alone with myself, even just briefly. A teeny, tiny little victory.

I take it anyway.

XXIII

That afternoon, I text Jo to make sure the meeting is still on with Ray, the girl he emailed me about. I had set it for after Willa's opening, thinking it could be another good distraction once my fake job was over. Now that the day's arrived, I wonder if it might be something more: a test case of how it feels to talk to someone in a controlled way.

He writes back to confirm, resending his organization's San Francisco address, and I reread the background information about Ray he had shared with me over email. I don't want her to have to recount it to me all in painful detail.

Ray came out as pansexual in the seventh grade, Jo wrote; she's gone back and forth on whether or not she might be nonbinary, and right now, she's leaning toward not. That wasn't such a big deal here as it might have been in other places. But then, relationship stuff got messy: Last year, when she was a sophomore, Ray broke up with her boyfriend and started dating a girl almost immediately.

The ex-boyfriend responded by posting the nudes she had sent him while they were together.

The pictures were reported and removed pretty quickly.

But a screenshot is faster than apps' trust and safety teams can ever be. And SF kids are pretty chill about a lot of things, but they're also kids, with all of the cruelty and carelessness that that entails. Ray knows—we all know—that those pictures will never entirely go away.

As I drive across the Bay Bridge at 4 p.m., I let the traffic distract me. I'm just going to have a conversation. My only job is to try to help in whatever way I can. Even if it feels too small to matter.

Jo has set us up in a small conference room; he gets us all water and then takes a seat. "So . . ." He looks between us. "Ray, I told you about Cassidy, and Cassidy, you've heard Ray's story. Ray has been thinking that getting involved in activism might help her cope with some of what she's gone through in the last year. Cassidy, I thought you might have some advice for her."

It's strange to try to match up what I know about Ray with the girl sitting across from me. I can't see any of what she's been through on her face. She hides herself, a bit like I suspect I hide myself. She's pale, with dark-brown hair pulled into a loose braid. She's pretty in the way all teenage girls are—fresh faced and too young and self-conscious to understand it.

"Sure, of course." I give Ray an encouraging smile, and she offers me one back. Teenagers can be such wildcards, but she seems engaged. She's willing to make eye contact, at least. "What were you thinking?"

Ray tells me about an essay she wants to write; we discuss the possible ways to frame it, if there are details she'd prefer to keep private. I encourage her to have a plan in place if she decides to share it or try to get it published somewhere: therapy sessions, friends on standby. "Speaking out can be important and healing," I tell her. "It can also feel like retraumatizing yourself. And it can be hard to tell how you'll feel until it happens, so it's important to be ready for whatever comes your way."

We've been talking for the better part of an hour, and I can feel Ray's attention slipping. She's been jiggling her foot; now she twists in her chair like she wants to get up but then doesn't. "Can I actually—can I ask you a question? In private?"

I look to Jo for confirmation; he shrugs as if to say, *Your call.*

I try to practice what I've just been preaching to Ray. I check myself to see how I feel about making this encounter more intimate. If my skin crawls at the idea of her asking about something she doesn't want to bring up in front of Jo—which, if I had to guess, would be about sex.

But I don't feel trapped or numb. And I know that as soon as I get back to my parents' house, I'm going to run myself a bath and get into it with a glass of wine. Go to sleep early. I'm tired, but I'm not worn out. I have a little more to give.

"Sure," I say.

Jo shuts the door behind him, and Ray looks at me. "When you've, uh, I assume you've, like, been with people. Since." Her cheeks are reddening with every word. "Is it—do you think about—if they're thinking about—"

I nod to let her know that I've gotten the gist of the question. "Okay if we make this about you instead of me?" I ask her. Boundaries. I think of Tilly and Ms. Palazzo.

She nods.

"There will be people who will know this about you and think about it always. And there will be people who will know this about you and will barely think about it at all. This fear you're having might not ever go away completely. But with the right person . . ." I sit straighter. "With the right person, you might stop worrying about it surprisingly quickly."

"Part of me really wants to just, like, prove that I'm totally over it. But every time I try . . ."

"You might not be ready yet. That's okay. It really is."

Ray shrugs like, *I guess*, and I'm pretty sure that wasn't an entirely satisfying answer. So I try another tactic. "Okay, here is one piece of wisdom I can share: There's no such thing as being all the way over it."

"Cool. So it never actually ends."

"No. It doesn't." I wish I could tell her something different: that we can escape our past selves and their worst mistakes and experiences. That you can outgrow trauma like an old coat. "But what if that's actually freeing? Because then you don't have to try so hard to get over it? It's not a race to the finish. Instead, it changes. And you change too. You have no idea how fucking much people can change."

The f-bomb coaxes a smile out of her. Predictable.

"Can I tell you something?" she asks. "I don't mean this

in a mean way. But, like, when Jo said I should talk to you, I honestly had no idea who you were."

Ray delivers this line with perfect, puzzled sincerity. And I can't help it: I throw my head back and laugh.

Of course she doesn't know who I am. She's sixteen. She would have been ten years old when my scandal broke, too young to care about sex or presidential politics. It's a welcome reminder that to some people, I'll always be notorious, but there are plenty of others who might never know my name unless they meet me. That I can't outrun my past. But my relationship to it—everyone's relationship to it—will keep evolving, shifting, and recalibrating.

On my way home, I don't listen to podcasts. I don't try to improve my mind or run away from it. I turn on music and let myself feel every mile of the drive: the distance between who I have been and who I want to try to be.

XXIV

On the train from Dulles to my apartment, I can feel every one of my pores opening up to sweat. The humidity is somehow even more overwhelming than I remembered. The air in my place is stale and much too warm. It already feels like somewhere I used to live.

But I haven't made any decisions yet, so I spend the weekend attempting to determine if this is somewhere I could be happy. I light a candle. I restock the fridge with my favorite foods. I get a bunch of flowers and put them in one of Willa's striped cups on my nightstand. I buy a plant that I know I'm going to end up killing; for now, its glossy green leaves make the place feel brighter. More alive.

Then, inevitably, it's Monday. My brain goes blank. I lean on muscle memory to put on a wrap dress, do my makeup, start my commute. I've made this particular trip thousands of times: during heat waves and rainstorms, hungover and underslept. On days when I was excited to get going and ones when I thought I would rather sink into the earth and die than check my email.

When I open my laptop, my inbox is a deluge, but there's

no time to deal with it. The first thing on my agenda this morning is a meeting with my boss, Patricia. Something about walking across the threshold jars me loose from the web of routine I've been caught in since I woke up.

The first time I stepped into this room was so long ago. I was a different person then.

I sit in the chair across from her and wait a moment while she finishes typing and hits *send* before turning to me. "Cassidy. Welcome back."

"Thank you. And thank you again for suggesting the time off. I don't think I realized how much I needed it until . . . well, until I did."

"I'm glad to hear that you were able to rest." She smiles, but I can tell she's looking me over, trying to see through my facade. To suss out if the cracks she saw a month ago have mended themselves or not.

Finally, I know the answer. "I didn't end up doing much resting," I start. "But I did do some thinking. And I think—I know—I'll always be grateful to you and KIB for taking me on. You all believed in me when no one else did. When I'm not sure I believed in myself." I take the deepest, longest breath. Then I let it out. "But I think it's time for me to move on."

I wait to see how the decision hits me: if I feel a flood of panic and regret. But I just feel . . . light. Like I've finally put down a backpack I've been hauling around—the kind so big and awkward that it's hard to sit or stand. I'll always be Cassidy Weaver: Before and After. But being her doesn't have to be my job anymore. I've earned the right to try something else. And finally, my desire to move forward has outstripped my fear of the unknown.

"I'm sad that you'll be leaving us, but I also—I can't say I'm shocked." Patricia gives me a conspiratorial smile. "I'm excited to see what you do next. You were so impactful to the organization during your time here, Cassidy."

Hearing that in the past tense is a relief.

From there, we move on to logistics. Instead of two weeks, I'm going to stay on for a month, to give them time to hire someone new and give me a chance to get everything sorted for whoever that is.

It turns out that, with an end date in mind, the work is much more bearable. In late September, I do one last event, something we scheduled a year ago. It's a conference for DC educators. I feel the usual knot of guilt and dread gathering in my stomach as I look out over the audience. I don't want to be responsible for telling everyone in attendance how to stop people from being assholes. Teachers probably know more about it than I do, anyway. But I share my story for a public audience, one last time. About how it felt to have the world's eye turn toward me and tell me I was scum. And about how it feels to keep trying to believe that that isn't true.

AFTER

XXV

I spend the next four weeks busy. Planning. Packing. Having goodbye brunches with friends I haven't kept up with nearly as well as I should have. Freaking out about whether or not I'm making the right call.

But most of all, I think about Leon. At first I try to resist it, to shut out the thoughts of his capable ease and quiet confidence. Images of his dimple and his laugh and his forearms. Memories of his hands in my hair and his mouth on mine. But after a while, I give up. There's no use in pretending that I'm over him.

At first the memories just feel cruel, like evidence of everything I was too broken to fix or keep. But once I stop fighting them, they take on a different quality. Slowly, gradually, they become something else: a story about how I tried to change and grow. About allowing myself to feel something thrilling and challenging for the first time in a long time.

When I finally tell Tilly about Leon, we agree that that night, I needed to turn him down. I needed this time to myself, away from him, to sort through things on my own terms. But as my time in DC draws to a close and I get closer and closer to something new, I keep wanting him to be a part of it. As I shed so many things, he's the one I don't want to shake.

When I arrive back in Berkeley, early Halloween decorations are up, houses outfitted with twelve-foot skeletons in Niners jerseys and yard signs campaigning for the upcoming election. Cooper's wedding has come and gone, and I was mostly able to avoid coverage of it. Yesterday I ignored a request for an interview with *Vanity Fair*, a piece about the afterlives of political mistresses. "A chance to tell your story," the email said, and I actually laughed.

I'm trying not to make too many decisions too quickly, but I have a loose plan in place: I'll stay with my parents for a semester while I take classes at a local community college and see if psychology is something I might be interested in pursuing more seriously. I'll work part-time for Willa, save up money, and hope to figure out the next steps by the spring. When I told Tilly that I might maybe follow in her footsteps, she chuckled. Encouragingly.

As soon as I drop my bags, I head straight to Willa's shop, eager to see it in action on a regular afternoon. There's one customer idly browsing the mugs and a couple inquiring about hand-building workshops. I introduce myself to the guy working the register and then head toward the back in search of Willa.

SQUARE WAVES

But three strides later, I see them. The paintings. I know immediately they're Leon's work. Simple wooden frames hold representations of the coast that emanate his particular energy. Views of the city as seen from a skateboard, a bike, a surfboard. Impressed with his surroundings but not overwhelmed by them.

I take them in as a group and then start to interrogate them, one by one. They're not perfect; there are bits of sloppy brushwork, places where his technique isn't quite there yet. But they're so—god, they're just so—

"Aren't they awesome?" says a voice from behind me. Willa has emerged from the back and caught me looking. "They arrived a few weeks ago."

"They're really special."

Willa plants her feet beside mine, and for a minute, we just . . . stand there. Admiring.

"Do you want to talk about it?" she asks.

"I want to hear how your first few months of girlbossing are going."

"Hard. So hard." Willa scuffs her toe against the floor. "But good too. So good. I'm glad I did this."

"Okay, well, let's get out of here." I look around, feigning like we're being spied on. "So you can tell me all about it."

We head to a coffee shop down the street, the one with the good donuts. We split their last glazed.

Willa eats her half and tells me about the ups and downs: that a Big Sur hotel reached out about vases for their restaurant, and of course they want them ASAP. How the first electrician she hired did a bad job, so she's looking for a second one. Bills are piling up slightly faster than she can pay them; holiday shopping season can't come quickly enough. But still, there's pride in her voice. She's tackling each of these obstacles head-on. No hand-wringing. She's just . . . doing it.

She mentions Leon a few times in passing, and each time, my heart leaps. Despite all of my DC ponderings, he and I haven't been in touch since I shut him down and walked away at the opening. I've wanted to wait until we could talk in person.

Willa must see it on my face, because after the fourth name-drop, she interrupts herself. "Ask," she says.

"Ask what?"

"About him. I know you want to."

"We don't need to—"

"Please. Do you know how many times he's almost asked me about you? I'm desperate for the two of you to finally actually get out of your own ways. And out of mine."

"You've been a very good friend."

"Don't I know it. Anyway. Ask."

There're a couple of napkins on the table; I fidget with the edge of one, tearing it into tiny strips. "I don't even know if I have a question for you. I mean, I assume he's . . . still Leon?"

"He is still Leon."

"And he—you think he might be open to hearing from me?"

"If the way he reacted when he overheard me saying your name the other day is any indication, then yes." Willa takes the napkin out of my hands. "I have to go to the bathroom. Don't do anything rash while I'm gone, okay?"

I nod. And I don't do anything rash. I don't go running out onto the street to make a big gesture or anything, anyway. But I do pull out my phone. I type *Hi* and then *Sorry* and then *Hahaha this is awkward*. Delete, delete, delete. I have so much I want to say, and none of it is appropriate for a text box. This is exactly why I've been putting this off.

Finally, I land on *I'm back in town and would love to see you* and hit *send*.

I don't see his message until I'm back in my car. *Okay*, Leon responded.

Tomorrow afternoon?

That works.

Which only leaves the question of where. A car honks to let me know that they'd like me to hurry up and hand over my space, which means I don't have time to overthink it. I had an idea back in DC. I follow that instinct now. *Meet me at Ocean Beach?*

XXVI

It's a gloriously clear and sunny day when I pull into the parking lot. It seems like a shift of surfers is just coming off the water; they're rinsing off boards and pulling off wetsuits, eyeing me with a look that says, *This spot is locals only, babe*. It's weird to remember that I am a local again, at least for the time being.

I make my way down to the sand. The ocean is in full force, rising high and crashing hard, much bigger than it was in Marin. Salt and spume give the wind extra bite.

I'm slightly early; a few minutes later, Leon arrives exactly on time. From where I'm sitting, I can see him making his way toward me, nodding hi to some of the guys he sees on his way. There's no question that Leon is from around here.

He's wearing baggy khaki pants and a thick wool sweater. A knit beanie pulled down over his shaggy waves. But I can see the shape of his body moving underneath his clothes, and the sight of it still makes my pulse pick up.

When he's close enough for us to hear each other, he stops. Both hands are in his pockets. He doesn't smile, but he doesn't look mad, exactly. Just curious. "What are we doing here?" he asks.

"You offered to teach me how to surf. When we were driving to Stinson. And I was wondering—I was wondering if the offer still stands."

Leon's face cycles through a dozen emotions, too quickly for me to capture any of them. He barks out a laugh. "You want to learn to surf?"

"I want a lot of things. I thought we could start there."

Leon starts walking; I scramble to my feet and fall into step beside him.

"How long are you back for?" he asks.

"Indefinitely."

He nods. Looks out at the waves. I wonder what he can read in them. What he's gleaned from so many hours spent watching them come and go.

"Listen, I'm just going to say some things, and you can decide how you feel about them. Last time we talked, you brought up Cooper. And how—how I'm afraid that other people will hurt me. And that's true, obviously. But the thing is, Leon—" I force a deep breath. "Even more than that, I'm afraid of hurting myself. The last time I chose someone, it was such a catastrophic mistake. For a long time, I would do anything not to open myself up to pain like that again. But being with you, and then not being with you, made me realize that it's holding me back in ways I don't like. It's keeping me from trying things. From being willing to just . . ." I gesture to the expanse in front of us, hoping it will convey what I can't.

"You can't learn at Ocean Beach," Leon says, keeping his face neutral. "The waves here are tough, and the culture—it's never gonna happen."

"We can go somewhere else."

"And it's fucking cold in there now. Colder than it was in August. Getting colder every day."

"I'll buy a wetsuit."

"And I'm not—" Leon stops. Turns toward me. He's standing between me and the shoreline, and his body blocks some of the wind, a perfect little shelter. "Are you serious, Cassidy?"

"I'm very serious."

For a long moment, we just look at each other. I can see Leon at fourteen: a kid, brash and charming, grabbing everyone's attention in class. How he mellowed into adolescence, withdrew into his own brand of perfectionism. And then him at Willa's: his hands shaping clay and sorting through cables and wires. Wrapping fragile ceramics. Touching me with the same reverent care.

I hope he can see all of my past selves. And the present one too.

"Okay, you're serious, about surfing. And what about us?"

"I'm serious about you too. If you'll let me be."

He considers this. "We're still gonna argue," he says. "I feel like that's a guarantee."

"Absolutely."

"And I might disappoint you again. That seems likely, in fact."

"Well, I'll definitely freak out again. That's my guarantee.

I'm never not—I'm working on it. But I—I really, really want to try."

I extend my hand toward his.

At last, one hand emerges from a pocket, and Leon slides his fingers through mine. Squeezes. The contact is a gentle hum of electricity: not a shock or a startle. Just the feeling that *this is right*.

"You've always made me want to try," he says softly.

"Yeah. Me too. I think that, somehow, we're good together."

"One of the many annoying things about you," he says, wearing that teasing smirk of his, "is how often you get things right."

I'm smiling so hard it hurts. "Look who's finally figuring that out."

Leon lets go of my grip and ruffles a hand through my hair. I pretend to hate it, but my body gives me away, and I lean into the touch. His palm slips down, cups my cheek. I can feel every one of his calluses: evidence of his willingness to put in the work, his openness to change.

I tilt my head to press a kiss onto his jaw. I can feel the slight shiver that goes through him when I do.

"Cassidy." His voice is rough, and I know we're both feeling more than we can say. But it has always been like that between us. Bigger feelings than either of us was ready to contend with: Rivalry, irritation, lust, tenderness. Maybe love.

I take the last step forward so that we're pressed together from head to toe.

"This, right here, feels perfect," I say, inhaling the scent of him.

Leon holds my face with both hands.

"Fuck perfect, Cass. This is better. This is us." And then he puts his mouth on mine and cracks me open, the way that only he can.

Keep riding the Cassidy and Leon wave: Read the book's epilogue *and* prologue (high school rivalry brought to life!), sip from Willa's striped cups, and listen to Charlie Blake's latest: a new single inspired by Cassidy's evolution. Scan here or visit 831stories.com/squarewaves.

ACKNOWLEDGMENTS

Thank you to Claire Mazur and Erica Cerulo, again and always. Thank you also to Larissa Pienkowski for your edits and Sanjana Basker and Maurene Goo for sensitivity reads. And thank you to everyone else at 831 for your help in making this book happen—in style, naturally.

Thank you to Kate Heller for always being down for an adventure, in the Bay and everywhere else. Thank you to Alex Kain for taking me to Berkeley Bowl and for twenty years (!!) of friendship. Thank you to Preston Hershorn and Sam Tooley for hosting a perfect dinner and for your notes on the neighborhood. Sorry I couldn't work in any LISTSERV drama or stray chickens. Maybe next time . . .

Thank you again to my own Tillys: Linda, Jenny, and Sophie. Thank you to my Lexapro prescription. SSRIs are life-saving medicine, and getting healthy will not keep you from making art if that's what you want to do.

Thank you, Mir. You've read the book, you know why.

Thank you, Mom, for the same reason.

ABOUT THE AUTHOR

ALEXANDRA ROMANOFF is a journalist, a cultural critic, and the author of *Big Fan*, which *Vogue* described as "political intrigue with a side of spine-tingling romance." She has written three young-adult novels under Zan Romanoff, and she also cohosts the podcast *On the Bleachers*, which examines the intersection of sports and pop culture. She lives and writes in LA.

ALSO FROM 831 STORIES

Big Fan by Alexandra Romanoff

Hardly Strangers by A.C. Robinson

Comedic Timing by Upasna Barath

Set Piece by Lana Schwartz